A F*CKERY OF FAE
AND FATE

A.J. BRAUN

CONTENTS

1. A Perfectly Good Wedding ... 1
2. One of Those Reverse Harem Books ... 14
3. Her Special Power is Thinking Dicks are Disgusting ... 29
4. Why are All These Men Wanting to Mate Me? ... 37
5. An Unnaturally Girthy Member ... 46
6. Introverts Don't Like Talking to People ... 54
7. You'll be Charged a Small Harassment Fee ... 65
8. Nothing Better than Free Entertainment and Butter ... 77
9. Anyone Want Some Bar-b-qued Winged Men for Dinner? ... 85
10. Ripe for the Picking ... 95
11. Butter & Barmaids Festival ... 102

Acknowledgments ... 107
About the Author ... 109

Map

Fae Realm
The Dark Lands
Fae Realm #2
Gulf of Mexico

1

A PERFECTLY GOOD WEDDING

My dragon and I weren't a typical bounty hunter pair.

We were never hired to take down the sorcerer who accidentally turned himself into a people-eating kraken in his attempt to cure the disease killing his daughter. Nor were we picked to take out the shady mobs making kingdoms into their personal gold stockpiles. We never even got the chance to join the other bounty hunters in squashing the cursed banshee regime (otherwise known as CBR) bent on scaring people to death instead of just *warning* them of death—had something to do with tax increases on their caves if I remember correctly.

And the only reason we never got *those* bounties was because my dragon and I were always assigned one type: killing magical immortal men who abducted young women.

According to the bounty hunter guild, we were the only ones who wouldn't immediately get on our knees and suck their dicks because they flashed a wink or rolled their sleeves up to their forearms.

So it was our job to save the suckers who did.

"We should be there by now," I shouted at my dragon, the wind whipping against my ears. My goggles took the brunt of the low-hanging clouds' moisture as I squeezed my thighs against my dragon's saddle.

It'd been a week since we'd gotten this job, the Blossom Court a further journey from our guild compared to other fae realm destinations. And one whole week was way too much time for shit to get out of hand.

Not to mention, the job was in the opposite direction of the Butter and Barmaids Festival, which we were *not* going to miss this year.

"Benny!" I shouted louder.

Still no response.

I rolled my eyes, shifting my thoughts into our mental bridge and knocking hard on his scaled mental wall. It fell away like shattered glass.

Arbentaliathoxian, I said sternly into his mind, *I know you heard me.*

Well, well, look who it is! Benny replied. **Using my full name, no less. It's great to hear from you too, Rhema. How's the ride?**

Get us lower, Benny. I can't see a damn thing.

Can't you just enjoy yourself for once? It's always Benny, veer left, or Benny, go higher—

Lower, I stated. *Now.*

Sheesh, even more demanding than usual.

Just follow my orders.

He laughed, **Does extra grumpy Rhema need a song to lift her spirits?**

I took a deep breath, biting my cheek so hard blood trickled onto my tongue. *We're not doing this right now.*

Oh, it's definitely time for a song.

A sharp turn threatened my balance. Readjusting my feet in the stirrups, I flexed my thighs and bent lower to avoid the gusts.

Benny, if we don't get to the Blossom Court in time, this new fae guy is going to have the princess under his spell. If that happens, it'll be nearly impossible to deliver her back to her kingdom in one piece.

Can't this guy turn into a moose or something?

I don't care if he can turn into a leviathon. We need the coin, or we won't make it to the Butter and Barmaids Festival.

Benny flapped his wings a beat too fast, the jolt causing me to slam onto the saddle. Good thing my ass was used to the pain after all these years.

Rhemy, what have I said about using fear tactics to make me fly faster? We'll get this job done lickity split—as per usual—grab our delicious horde of gold, and then I can eat ALL the butter I want and you can make out with barmaids until you lose count.

I'm there for the ale, Benny. Barmaids are just a... plus.

A BIG plus if my memories from two years ago serve right. Or you could even invite Rosanna—I bet you two could have a LOT of fun together.

If by fun you mean I'd finally be able to beat the shit out of her, then yeah, I guess it'd be a ton of fun.

Ah, still holding that grudge after an entire year. Doesn't that get exhausting?

Can we not talk about the person solely responsible for ruining our chances at getting monster bounties? Gods, just get us out of this damn clou—

Whose wings glint and glitter
With a bitter bitch-sitter
As they gracefully flitter?
Arbentaliathoxian!

I groaned as he finally lowered us out of the cloud, the moisture beading off my black leathers. Green meadows and shining lakes gleamed underneath our wake; the beauty of the Blossom Court would be difficult to rival if it wasn't for the saccharine sweet air that came with it: a blatant reminder the fae realm was dangerous.

Especially to unassuming humans.

"Over there." I redirected our path with a quick tug of the leather reins.

Benny obeyed, continuing his song as we dipped lower to the ground. A shining white building burned my eyes, the circular structure pillowed in a flowery meadow surrounded by a sprawling forest.

To my horror, a small crowd was gathered in its backyard.

Is it just me, or is that a wedding? Benny asked.

Shit.

One kiss and that fae would have the princess in his clutches for good. If we didn't kill him and return the princess, our coin purse would be empty, which meant we couldn't even *buy* our tickets to the Butter and Barmaids Festival.

Faster, Benny!

Apparently, a gold dragon diving straight for a wedding procession didn't bother people, which was surprising considering Benny measured about four carriage lengths. I supposed the fae realm was used to mythical creatures soaring through their skies.

Or, whatever was happening in the ceremony was distracting enough.

Maybe she hasn't said yes yet, Benny huffed in excitement. *Maybe we'll arrive right as they ask—*

"Are there any objections to this matrimony?" the officiant asked, a woman clad in green priestly robes.

Before it could go any further, I jumped off Benny's back. He soared back into the sky while I slammed to the ground, landing on one knee.

Pain shot through my entire leg.

"*Fuck,*" I whispered.

I told you to stop doing that, Benny said, *awful for your knees.*

Stop worrying about my knees and just wait for my signal.

Stumbling to my feet, I wiped off purple petals stuck to my black leathers. The springtime bloom smelled even worse down here. A deep cough from somewhere in the crowd reminded me how deathly quiet it'd become.

In front of me stood the princess, her brown hair tied up in an intricate array of knots and frills. She looked to be no more than five feet tall and was swimming in a horrifyingly gaudy wedding dress with so many ruffles it threatened to eat up her entire body. If she was beautiful, it was hard to tell. On the altar stood the fae prince, his long black hair, chiseled jaw, and flaming gaze a sight that made me want to roll my eyes.

"I object," I said, raising a hand, "so, if we could hurry this up, I'd like to get the princess back to her kingdom as quickly as possible."

"I beg your pardon," the priestess started, "but who do you think you are?"

"Arwel," the princess said, her voice graceful and smooth as she turned to the fae prince, "what's going on?"

"Get out of my court," the fae man—Arwel—snarled, "she became mine through a legitimate bargain." He turned to the princess. "I knew she was my home the moment I saw her."

The princess gasped, a pretty pink flushing her stained cheeks.

Gag me.

He really lays it on thick, doesn't he? Benny commented.

More than most. Are you ready for phase two?

Oh, I'm always ready for phase two.

Good. Because by the looks of this, it's going to get ugly.

"Look," I replied to the prince, "I really don't want to have to resort to a fight with you. Just a clean picking and then everyone here can be spared. So, hand over the girl and your head, and we'll be through this before lunchtime."

"My head as well?" Arwel questioned. "And you think you and your dragon can defeat me, the Prince of Spring? You don't realize just how far over your head you are, do you, woman?"

"*Woman?*" I scoffed, "What the hell is this, the dark ages?"

Before he could respond, a sudden wind whipped across my face, loud and stormy, as if a thunder cloud had warped into the middle of the aisle. I grabbed my axe and turned around to see a haze of blue-and-white mist forming into a tall masculine figure with pointed ears, a white coat lined with silver thread, and a chill so frigid the petals withered into frozen droplets.

"I object on behalf of Princess Gwenyth's best interests," the winter fae grinned.

So this princess had *two* fae vying for her. How typical. Can't manage to find women in their own age bracket, so they pursue the young ones.

I had a sudden urge to wretch.

"Now, Arwel, let's not get into our usual bickeri—" the white-haired fae paused, seeming to notice I was standing before him with an axe. "Wait, who are you?"

Phase two! Benny shouted into my mental bridge.

Hold on, not yet.

Too late.

A cone of fire burst in front of me, the heat burning my face. The white-haired fae went up in flames, screeching like a bird. Feathered wings started to sprout from his shoulders, his eyes glowing a deep blue, and claws protruding from his nails.

But the guy didn't stand a chance against Benny's fire, fae or not.

Dragons could burn through anything.

"Gwenyth!" he screamed through the barrage of heat, "*No, we didn't even get the chance to fuck—!*"

The flames stopped as soon as they came, and all that was left of the pretty fae was a pile of ash.

"Trefor!" the princess screamed.

Then, the real noise started. Yells and shouts erupted, wedding guests tumbled out of their seats, plumes of smoke rose into the air, and a monstrous roar rumbled into the ground.

"Gods, it's like they've never seen bounty hunters before," I remarked.

Alright Benny, I spoke into his mind, *time to clean up and save this princess.*

Ass up. Face down. Can't lose!

No. I pointed at him. *No, no, no, we are NOT making that our catch phrase.*

Why are you pointing at me? It's YOUR phrase, and I want it to be our "thing". You know? Something people can remember us by.

I was drunk during that job!

And it was truly one of your finest moments yet, Rhemy dearest.

Laughing, Benny swooped above me, raining fire on any fae attempting to grab the princess, careful to avoid hitting her. Smoldering flames erupted, burning flowers, chairs, and grass.

"Why can't he let that memory die?" I muttered.

"We can't get the dragon, but we can end her!" the priestess officiant yelled, pointing at me.

A group of armored fae sprinted for me; I arced my axe through the air. Widening my stance, I readied for what would be their inevitable moves. Magic was predictable: a crutch. It was obvious they couldn't beat me in a straight-laced melee combat, so they'd have no choice but to wield their power.

Each fae wisped away through mirrors of smoke—traveling through a dimensional space I couldn't see.

Lucky for me, I had a dragon who could read their thoughts.

One from above, two from your left, and one on your right, Benny chimed in my mind.

Cries erupted as the fae appeared through their smoky gates. my axe swooping in the pattern Benny gave me and slicing clean through each of their torsos. Warm blood splattered my face, their bodies littering the wedding aisle and swords clanking to the ground.

The princess shrieked as she dashed behind one of the pillars at the altar, her hair falling into long brown curls.

"Uh, sorry, just don't look," I encouraged her.

A blond-haired fae charged me, but just as he was about to slice his sword through my heart, he wisped away. I didn't need Benny for this one.

Were fae males powerful? Yes.

Tactically smart? Not even close.

My axe crunched through the wide-eyed fae that appeared behind me.

"You *bitch*," he choked out.

"Yeah, I've never heard that one before."

"You ruined... a perfectly good... wedding..." He slumped to the ground, mouth and eyes agape.

"Those are your last words?" I asked the dead body. "I would've gone with something more vengeful like 'rot in hell' or 'damn you' or at least something mildly interesti—"

A sharp blow knocked me to the ground as a scream pierced my eardrums. I let my shoulder take the hit before rolling up to stand. Before me was the priestess, her dark-green robes singed with fire, the sobbing mess of a princess crouched behind her at the altar.

"You're going to burn for this," the priestess yelled.

I smiled.

"Benny?" I tapped into his mental bridge, *Can you finish this priestess for me? I need to get the princess before she devolves into a traumatized puddle.*

It would be my honor.

I waved farewell at the priestess. She gave me a quizzical look before going up in flames.

I owe you some extra butter for that.

Yippee! Benny shouted as he continued his carnage.

Have you seen the fae prince? I asked.

Oh yeah, he's running towards the forest. But I burned him pretty bad, so it's more like a really sad wobble.

He's retreating? I laughed out loud. *Ok, new plan. You keep watch over the princess and I'll catch the prince.*

He's headed south. Have fun!

I took off sprinting. It felt good, my legs burning, adrenaline pumping strong and relentless through my muscles. Thirteen years of rigorous training was the reason I was bonded to the most powerful dragon in the land.

If only Benny didn't sing so fucking much.

Branches cut my face as the limping prince came into view. His black hair was caked in blood, fancy clothes burned to a crisp, and his whimpering sounded far more like a woodland creature than a fully-grown man.

"If you stop and meet your death with open arms, then you'll go down with dignity," I called.

But he only screamed as he kept hobbling forward.

Gods help me.

I caught up to him in a few strides and kicked the back of his knees, sending him to the ground. Sobbing, he turned on his back, hands held above his face.

"Please, spare me, Warrior," he cried.

"You fucking cheated your way into a bargain for that princess. What have you to say for yourself?" I demanded.

Tears ran down his pathetic cheeks. "I don't give a damn about the girl. Please, just don't take me back to her. I'll do anything!"

"You don't want to go back to the princess?"

"I'm not talking about her!" he yelled, "I know I wasn't supposed to leave for another few hundred years, but I couldn't stand that woman any longer! The warden offered us a way out; I wasn't going to squander such a brilliant pass of luck. Please, just let me live in these woods. Spare me!"

Confusion pulled at my mind. "What in the hells are you talking about?"

He didn't respond. Instead, his cries turned from pitiful whimpers to low and rumbling mewls. Horns poked from his head and fur sprouted on his face, neck, and hands. Gold light consumed him as he began to shape-shift.

But it was a pointless escape attempt on his part. My job was to kill him and return the princess.

And I was done wasting time.

Before he could run, I slammed my axe into his chest. A low moan came from his outstretched jaw, his moose horns fully formed, the lower half of his body covered in fur and ending in hooves. His blue eyes faded into a pale white.

Benny, I pushed into his mind, *any idea why this guy talked as if he'd been imprisoned somewhere?*

Why don't you ask him?

Uh, can't really do that anymore.

Ah, good 'ol axe to the chest.

I should've just dragged him back with us and tortured the information out of him.

Does Rhemy need to get lunch soon?

You're missing the point, I retorted, *and, ok yeah, lunch would be good too.*

As I trudged back to the bloodied wedding ceremony, I ignored the creeping sense I killed him preemptively. But this was the job, and keeping him alive as a moose wouldn't have benefited us anyways.

All that was left of the ceremony was the princess shaking on the altar, her knees tucked into her chest. In the aisle, Benny sat on an array of chairs—crushing them, of course—while the purple flower petals mingled with blood.

"Well," I said as I approached the princess, "that certainly could've gone a bit smoother. But, I'm glad we got here in time.

Your parents are extremely worried about you; I mean to get you back to your kingdom within the week."

But the princess didn't respond, her eyes locked to her shaking hands.

Rhema, she's in shock, Benny said into my mind.

I know, I know, I chided back.

It was easy to forget others weren't used to this kind of battle scene. If anything, it bewildered me that some people grew up in peaceful forests or by calm rivers. My life had been run by war ever since I could remember.

Slowly, I kneeled in front of her. "Let's start off by fetching you some water, getting you some foo—"

A sharp sting ran across my face as the princess slapped me.

"How *dare* you," she screamed.

Working my jaw back and forth, I gave her a flat smile. "Oh, you mean how dare I save you from a group of predatory men who outwitted your father so they could fuck you and cage you? My sincerest apologies, Princess."

She shuddered, her tear-stained face splotched with pink and splattered with blood.

"I loved him," she whispered.

I couldn't help but chuckle. "Who? The one who ran away the moment everything went to shit? Yeah, he seemed like a real catch."

"Isn't it enough that you killed him? Now you mock him, too?"

"He literally said he didn't give a damn about y—"

Rhema, Benny warned.

I bit my tongue. "Look, Princess, you can either stay here and grow old with these corpses, or you can return home to your family with us."

"My name's Gwenyth."

I sighed. "*Gwenyth.* We're hungry and I bet you are too. So let's head over to a tavern and then get you back to your kingdom."

Gwenyth said nothing. Instead, she avoided my gaze and stared at the billowing flames in our wake.

Very smooth, Benny ground into our mental bridge.

What? I'm starving, and she's taking forever.

I knew we should've brought snacks. But what did you tell me? No, Benny, these little strips of dried meat will do me just fine.

Can you stop talking for two seconds?

Maybe I should talk to her.

And scare her even more with your disembodied voice popping into her head? She's obviously never seen a dragon before, let alone talked with one. There's a reason your species has etiquette laws about this shit.

Fine, but you're going to need to actually be nice.

I bit back a curse I wanted to throw into Benny's mind; cursing wouldn't do me any good. I needed this princess to come with us, and I wasn't going to wait all day and night for her to decide.

"I'm sorry," I said, gently placing my hand on her shoulder.

She flinched, but she didn't back away.

I continued, "I can tell he meant a lot to you and that us coming in and, well, killing everyone was a bit of a shock."

"A bit of a shock?" she replied, voice raised. "Is that what you call this?"

I flared my nostrils.

Fuck it.

Before she could react, I pinched the soft muscle at the base of her neck, just above her collarbone; she fell limp into my arms. I couldn't help but notice how much the dress had hidden the curve of her tits.

Beautiful and vicious. Great.

She's going to love you for that one, Benny chimed in.

I'm counting on it, I drawled back, *let's just get to a tavern. We* can let her recover for a few hours before riding back to her kingdom. Then, we'll get our coin and still have an extra few days to make it to the Festival.

And I can test out more of my songs with drunk humans!

As long as you actually get everyone's permission this time AND I'm blacked out, I mumbled.

I climbed onto Benny's back and placed the unconscious princess in front of me, tying a rope around us. She didn't wake as we flew away, leaving the Blossom Court covered in blood—but something in my chest kept eating away at me, like whatever the fae prince had said about being "let out" wasn't just a passing comment taken by the wind. And godsdamnit because if there was one thing Benny and I always attracted, it was problems.

We'd have to be vigilant on our journey to this princess' kingdom, or else we might have to deal with something even worse than two cocky fae princes.

But what that could be?

I didn't have a fucking clue.

2

ONE OF THOSE REVERSE HAREM BOOKS

PUFFY CLOUDS SCATTERED below us as the cool wind swept through my half-shaved hair. The princess—Gwenyth—who smelled like an entire bush of peonies was, after three days of persistent glaring, finally slumped against me asleep. Thankfully, she'd be out of our hair soon enough once returned to her kingdom.

Benny didn't even need to flap his scaly wings, the breeze guided us back to the human realm like it wanted us to get to the Butter and Barmaids Festival on time. Oh gods, I couldn't wait. Benny could sing to a crowd instead of *just* me, I could drink bottomless pints of ale for five days straight, and maybe I'd even meet someone and, well, have some fun.

Damn, it'd been a while since I'd slept with anyone. I missed being between a woman's legs. And as much as I hated to admit it, there was one woman I especially missed, sliding my hands up her hard stomach and caressing the swell of her breas—

Oh my gods, I'm going to be sick.

Flinching, I ground my teeth. *Benny, what have I said about sneaking into my mental bridge?*

You think I wanted to hear all that? he whined. *You're practically shouting about how much you love boobs like a yodeler on top of a canyon.*

I wasn't even thinking about boobs.

You were about to.

No I wasn't.

Uh, yeah, you were. Benny paused, followed by a small obnoxious hum. *You miss Rosanna, don't you?*

I scoffed. *The woman who stole our rightful guild spot as monster bounty hunters? Not a fucking chance.*

And you say I'm the dramatic one, Benny groaned.

Do you even hear yourself? We could be out there slicing monsters and saving entire villages, but instead we're stuck saving silly little princesses from idiotic men. Doesn't that piss you off?

Nope! He grinned. *Monsters are so ten years ago. Besides, I like that we get to save people like Gwenyth.*

I glared at the sleeping princess, cursing her naturally rosy cheeks and soft pouted lips. Nothing more annoying than a pain-in-the-ass being beautiful.

Well, as far as I'm concerned, Rosanna can go get consumed by one of those poisonous gas monsters for all I care.

Do you smell smoke?

Smoke?

Because I think your leather trousers are on fire.

I groaned. *What are you, seven?*

Seven hundred and eighty-three years old, to be precise.

Tell me again why you change your age every time it's brought up?

It's one of my favorite games!

You're an idiot.

And you miss Rosanna.

Benny, we fucked once and then she stabbed me in the back. End of story.

He gasped. *It's like she's a bounty hunter or something?*

I hate you.

Admit it. You miss her.

I miss boobs.

You miss her.

I miss legs.

Rhemy, why can't you just let the past stay in the past?

My insides suddenly froze, any warmth in my face gone. Memories surged from war-torn years and a love I once had...

...lost.

I'm done talking about this.

Just because you lost someone you loved once doesn't mean it'll happen agai—

I said I'm done, Benny, alright?

A small silence spanned between us, gusts of wind brushing past my ears.

He sighed. **Fine. What does my four hundred and seventy-seven year old ass know anyways?**

Why can't you just be normal and say your actual age?

My thoughts were interrupted as Gwenyth woke up—elbowing me in the boob with her bony little elbow while she was at it. Air rushed out of my lungs.

"Stop holding me so tight," she yelled over the wind.

I loosened my grip. "You could've just *asked*, you know?"

She turned. "And you could've just let my fiancé live instead of *murdering* him."

Gritting my teeth, I refused the instinct to crack her spine in half. "Oh yeah, your little prison break fae prince really seemed to care for you when he ran away."

"He didn't escape from a *prison*. He was the ruler of the Blossom Court and you killed him in cold blood. You're the criminal here."

"He's the one who said he was let out by a warden." I paused, trying to keep the last bit of his pre-death confession to myself, but she'd insulted me enough these last few days that I didn't fucking care anymore. "*And* that he didn't give a shit about you."

Rhema, Benny scolded.

She won't believe it anyways, I replied.

The princess' gray eyes flashed. "Your lies are humorous to me."

"Who could've guessed that?" I chided.

When Gwenyth shifted in her seat, her wedding-dress ruffles poked my eye, a sharp sting causing me to bat away the unnecessarily hazardous material.

"I'm thirsty," Gwenyth said, crossing her arms.

"Can you just go back to snoring and drooling?"

"I said, I'm *thirsty.* And if you want my father's coin, then you'll want to make sure you get a five star review from me."

Maybe it *would've* been better if I'd just broke her slender little nec—

Alright, my turn to talk to her, Benny said.

Benny, no, I grumbled back, *we agreed no conversations with her.*

But it's been three entire days and you're just making it worse!

I am not.

Then give her a smile. Just one.

I'd rather die.

See? Besides, there's a lake just up ahead. It's the perfect time to take a water break and introduce myself!

I slapped my face. *Benny, please, by the mercy of all the gods, don't sin—*

The familiar high-pitched whine of Benny connecting all three of our mental bridges scraped along my eardrums, the princess flinching as she let go of the reins and covered her ears. She slipped, but I caught her around her waist. An unbidden memory flitted through my head: Rosanna's pleading brown eyes as she laced her fingers with mine, bucking her hips into me as I gripped her waist.

My face heated. Quickly, I doused the memory.

Gwenyth's gaze shot to me for a moment, her cheeks red and brows set in a firm glare.

Did she want me to let her drop out of the sky?

Maybe I'd let her next time, for both our sakes.

Gwenyth! Benny spoke into both our minds. *Oh I've been looking forward to formally introducing myself. Rhema thought it was best we not converse to make your travel less eventful.*

"What's happening?" the princess shouted.

I sighed. "Well, Princess, dragons can connect to our minds as easily as you're able to insult me. And even though dragons are supposed to only converse with their riders, my dragon's a bit rude."

Getting to know people isn't rude, Rhema.

It is when you just shove yourself into their weak mental bridge, I warned.

"How do I speak back to him?" she asked.

"Trust me, it's better if you don't."

She tried anyways, but all it sounded like were little grunts and huffs blowing in our mental bridges.

It's alright, Gwenyth, just speak out loud and I'll hear you just fine! Do you like music? Songs?

No singing, I interjected.

"In that case, I'd love a song," Gwenyth replied with a smirk, the closest thing I'd seen to a smile since we rescued her.

And so, to my dismay, Benny introduced himself.

Whose wings glint and glitter
With a bitter bitch-sitter
As they gracefully flitter?
Arbentaliathoxian!

Sunlight reflected off the glassy lake, Benny continuing to sing his damned chorus as we soared towards the water's shore. The princess bobbed her head as if she actually enjoyed his little performance.

With scales so astounding,
And great roar resounding,
Greatness surrounding,
Arbentaliathoxian!

We landed with a thud, squawking birds flitting to the sky and a layer of dust floating over the ground.

Arbentaliathoxian!
Arbentaliathoxian!
The paragon,
Of dragon son,
Arbentaliathoxian!

The princess clapped, and Benny hummed with satisfaction. Only a few waking moments with these two and I could tell this was going to be the nightmare I'd aimed to avoid.

The Butter and Barmaids Festival couldn't come soon enough.

"Alright, Princess, time to get your precious lake water." I slid off Benny's back and took her with me.

She screamed.

Her knees shuddered as we hit the ground, and she fell into my arms. Those small hands of hers slid from my collarbone to my chest. Eyes wide, she stared at me with an open mouth; I hadn't realized until now the small gap between her front teeth. I held her waist to keep her upright, that godsdamn heat rising in my face again. She looked almost... familiar.

What the fuck is happening?

Oh, does Rosanna have competition?

Benny, out of my head! Now!

His giggle faded out of my mind.

As if she heard my thoughts—which she *hadn't*—she quickly met me with a slap to both my arms and a shove that felt more like a light breeze than a person pushing me.

"I need privacy," Gwenyth stated.

I raised a brow. "To drink water?"

"To *bathe*. Thanks to you two, I've been covered in the blood of my friends for three whole days."

"Not our faults you weren't willing to bathe or take a change of clothes at the other inns."

"You were going to *watch* me, you pervert."

"Because I don't trust you to stay put, not because I want to actually see what's underneath all... *that*."

Her face flushed pink as her throat bobbed.

Something flashed in her eye—had I actually hurt her feelings? It's not like I'd meant it. Underneath all that dress, she was clearly beautiful, probably had a slender waist, wide hips, and tits that were perkier than they had any right to be.

I would sooner listen to Benny perform an entire concert than admit *those* thoughts.

"Let's not argue about logistics, hm? Besides, Princess, I'm more concerned about other things," I said quickly, ignoring the guilt suddenly eating away at my stomach, "like how you don't seem too shaken up about the whole murdering thing. I've rescued other women who can't even speak because they're in so much shock."

She ignored me and turned to Benny, "Please, Arbentaliathoxian? I just need a few minutes or my dress will be forever ruined; I want to have something to remember Prince Arwel by."

Of course, Princess, Benny sang into our minds.

Don't give into her antics, I growled.

But she's right! All that blood is really ruining her whole I-want-to-find-my-true-love princess vibes.

I don't give a shit what she looks like. We're on a tight schedule.

Oh, Rhema, beauty doesn't adhere to schedules.

Gwenyth patted Benny's snout, "Exactly. Thank you for understanding, Arbentaliathoxian."

He smiled and gave her a gentle snort. **Benny's just fine, Gwenyth.**

Two against one. And I thought my dragon was supposed to be on *my* side in all of this. But of course, the princess loved his singing—which meant she was a fan—so he'd do whatever the hells she wanted to keep her happy.

I glared at her. She offered a wide smile.

"Fine, Princess, go take your beauty bath. But we're leaving in ten minutes."

"So gracious of you," she drawled.

Benny and I flew to the other side of the lake. Gwenyth was nothing more than a small dot in the distance—but at least we could keep track of her. Eating a thin strip of dried meat, I plopped on the sandy shore while Benny licked his talons, which were oddly square-shaped instead of pointed.

"I thought you were supposed to get your talons sharpened the other day?"

Benny looked up mid-lick. *I did.*

Then how are you supposed to tear through flesh with those?

Rhema, it's called TRENDS. Sharp, pointy talons are out, square-cut talons are in. And social suicide is not on the menu.

You've got to be joking.

I don't expect you to understand culture, Rhemy. Speaking of your lack of understanding, you and this princess are getting along nicely, Benny chided.

Shut up, I groaned.

Remember what I said about letting the past be in the past?

Remember how she just played you like a fiddle to get what she wanted?

And now she trusts me, he retorted.

Narrowing my gaze, something wary stirred inside my chest. Between her sarcastic smiles and obvious manipulation of Benny's desire for fame, I couldn't stop wondering if she was up to something.

Maybe if you actually gave people a chance, you'd end up having more friends than just me.

I don't need friendship advice from y—

A large bird darted into the forest behind Gwenyth's bathing spot.

Did you see that? I asked.

Benny stopped licking himself. ***Looked like a really big bat.***

What a wise assessment from an ancient mythical creature.

I just call it as I see it, and it looked like a bat with luscious hair.

What? You know what, nevermind. Let's just go get Gwenyth before that thing causes any issues.

Uh oh.

My body froze. Gwenyth wasn't bathing anymore, in fact, she wasn't anywhere on the shoreline.

"Fuck." I swung onto Benny's back. "What were you saying about trusting her?"

Harsh wind threatened to throw me off as Benny shot across the lake. He drove up over the dense forest just as another bat-like creature darted through the sky.

No way that was coincidence.

Follow it and get your fire-breathing ready, I instructed Benny.

Rhema, you know I'm part of the Forest Conservation Society for Dragons! It's my sworn duty to protect these trees, not scorch them down. I even got elected treasurer last week.

I scrunched my eyes shut. *Was this before or after your fucking manicure?*

During! We've got a wonderful self-care budget. Makes meetings far more bearable.

I'm going to kill y—

Before I could finish my threat, he followed the creature into a clearing and landed with a heavy thud. Unsheathing my axe, I jumped off his back and waited for the dust to clear.

Twenty men wearing tight all-black clothing stood before us, their shirts each featuring a deep "v" that revealed their muscular pecks, and rolled-up sleeves that exposed their veiny forearms. Each of them had large leathery wings jutting out of their backs, all of them ending in sharp talons. In the middle of the group, Gwenyth stood with her chin held high. Her bloodied, poofy wedding dress was sopping wet as she grasped onto one of the bat-like men's bulging arms.

"I'm not going back with you two," Gwenyth announced, the winged man grabbing her waist and pulling her close, "these are Trefor's men and they've come to save me."

"Who the fuck is Trefor?" I questioned.

Oh, the other one who showed up at the wedding? Benny spoke into all our minds. *The one I drowned in flames? He had those really pretty blue eyes and some sexy feathered fae wings, which, to be honest Gwenyth—I totally get it.*

"Benny, now is *not* the time," I said, "Princess, let's just leave these winged men and we'll pretend this never happened, alright?"

"You don't understand," she yelled, "my father means to marry me off to a man I don't even know. I'm staying here. *I'm* choosing who I'm going to love. *I'm* choosing my destiny."

I sighed. "Sometimes love, much like destiny, isn't ours for the taking."

"Away from her!" one of the men said, stepping forward. "We came to rescue her from you."

"Oh yeah? And what are you going to do with her?"

The man's brows furrowed. He turned back to his fellow winged men. All of them murmured back and forth, some of them offering a shrug. Gwenyth's eyes widened.

"We, uh, we're going to mate her!"

"What?" Gwenyth shouted.

"That's right, we're all going to mate her, because she's ours and ours alone," the winged man announced, "she belongs to us from now until forevermore."

"Like shit I do," Gwenyth said, letting go of his arm.

But then, he grabbed her. And then another man grabbed

her. I stepped forward, a sudden burst of heat radiating up and down my chest.

"Get off me," she growled, "I'm not your mate!"

Another winged man stepped forward, also rippling with muscle, "It's true, Morpheus. You may say she's our collective mate, but we know only one of us can truly have her. And that one person is me."

Wow, this is like one of those harem books. Gwenyth's one lucky gal.

Benny, now isn't—wait, harem books?

Do you not follow my Goodscrolls account? Oh, Rhema, they're my favorite. I'll give you a great recommendation—nothing too intense though. Starting off easy is the smartest way to go.

A third winged-man rushed forward and drew his sword. "Touch her and you die, Elyan!"

Oh, but they haven't learned consent, have they? Enthusiastic agreement is key!

"Rhema! Benny!" Gwenyth struggled against the men pulling her back. "Help!"

Without another thought, I sprinted towards Gwenyth. The winged men erupted in roars and shouts, swords clanking and Gwenyth screaming in the fray of blood and muscles. Keeping my senses sharp, I dodged a sword and rolled away from a nasty punch.

Gwenyth's brown hair caught the sunlight in the sea of black wings, but before I could grab her, a winged man swooped in and took her, darting back to the lake. The other men stopped their fighting and followed with battle cries.

"Benny, the lake, now!" I yelled.

Grabbing onto the leather reins, I didn't have time to swing onto his back as we bolted upward. Branches scraped my face before we arced over the forest, hovering over the shoreline where Gwenyth cried in the middle of a battle scene.

If I grab Gwenyth, can you breathe your fire this time, or are you still going to be an environmentalist about it? I yelled into his mind.

Don't be silly, Rhemy, lakes aren't endangered.

I didn't even have time to roll my eyes as I dropped into the fray of men. Axe unsheathed, I swung and split one of the fae in half as he yelled some obnoxious phrase about mating with the princess during the Spring Solstice. Blood splattered all over me.

I dodged a sword aimed for my gut. Crunching my axe through that fae's middle, I finally found Gwenyth and wrapped my arms around her ribcage.

"I don't want to mate you!" she shouted.

"It's just me, Princess."

"*Rhema.*"

She didn't fight me as I dragged her away from the gory battle, heads rolling into the sand and bodies skewered to trees lining the shore.

Benny, I called through our mental bridge, *phase two!*

Coming right up!

Fire shot from his mouth, the heat so intense I covered Gwenyth with my body and threw us behind a bush. When the burning sensation on my leathers dissipated, I lifted my head. Gwenyth stared at me with wide tearful eyes. Her throat bobbed, and I didn't miss the way her gaze darted to my mouth before scrunching shut.

Alright, the sexy winged-men are dead, rest their seductive nonconsensual souls, Benny announced in our mental bridges, **but they smell really, really gross.**

Then let's get out of here, I replied, ignoring the way my heart pounded against my chest when Gwenyth burrowed her head into my neck. As we approached the shoreline, I let out a low whistle: Benny had burned them all to ash.

Job well done, I said.

Does that mean more butter for me? he asked.

It sure does.

Opening the small cold pack hung on my waist, I took out a few coin-sized butterballs and tossed them into the air. Benny slurped them up and sang a happy tune.

I swung onto his back, grabbing Gwenyth's outstretched hands and pulling her up in front of me. She was difficult to maneuver, her bloody wedding dress extra poofy from multiple rips and a broken hoop skirt.

"Sorry about this," I grunted as I ripped the sleeves. An array of ruffles fell from her dress.

She gasped, "Wait, don't ruin it!"

"I think it's too late for that."

Clutching my arm to keep from falling, Gwenyth squirmed while I tore another ruffle, but it didn't seem to change much. So I ripped another layer. Then another. And *another.* I swear to the gods, a whole seven minutes went by before her slender shoulders were visible. By the end, a litter of white ruffles and lace sat piled next to us like a snowstorm had passed.

For the finale, I unlaced her corset and broke the metal hoop skirt. She held onto me as she kicked it off her legs.

Damn. I'd been right about what she looked like underneath all that: fucking perfect, but that wasn't the worst part.

It was *who* she looked like.

"Oh," Gwenyth said with a trembling voice. "I didn't realize how difficult it'd been to breathe with all of that."

I shook my head, trying to recalibrate my thoughts so I knew I was talking to a scared princess, not my dead wife.

"Great, now I can see and you can fucking move," I remarked, hoping my voice sounded steadier than I felt, "now go ahead and grab Benny's reins with me. I'm going to hold on extra tight to you so you stay put, got it?"

She gave a small nod, her body shaking from shock.

Instinctively, I wiped a stray hair behind her ear before

wrapping my arm around her and pressing her back against my chest. Her breath hitched.

"Gwenyth," I started as Benny pushed off into the air, "how did you find those men?"

"I didn't. They found me."

"How?"

"I," she paused, turning to me, "I don't know."

I let out a troubled breath. *Benny, any idea where those winged men came from?*

No clue, he replied, **think it has to do with that fae prince's prison break?**

More than likely.

Want me to get on the line with Rosanna's dragon?

I loved and hated the way my body responded to hearing her name, like a wave of electricity zipping through my muscles. But it *wasn't* real feelings, just a natural desire to be fucked. And I knew this because even though the one time we did fuck was pure bliss—probably the best sex I'd ever had— that's all it was; the next day she had fucked me over in the I-will-never-trust-you-again kind of way.

Not to mention how I was caressing my dead wife's look-alike in my arms.

Gods, this was *not* how these bounty jobs usually went.

I think I'd rather fend off the hordes of winged men by ourselves, I replied.

But if we run into more of these guys, we might be more delayed, Benny whined. **If anyone knows what's happening, it's her.**

We'll figure it out on our own.

Rhemy, I need more butter balls and you promised we'd make it to the Festival so we can get them! Can't you just put your dramatic little feelings aside this once? For me?

He turned and his red eyes glinted with fresh-forming tears. Dammit. Why couldn't he be singing one of his grating songs instead of looking at me like I was bludgeoning his heart? In any case, he was right. We couldn't afford any more delays. I refused to miss the Festival for a second year in a row—I *earned* my five days of ale and women.

Besides, there was no way in all the hells and heavens I would go back on a promise I made to Benny.

Fine, I finally said, *see if she's able to meet at the village we're headed to. I don't trust you and her dragon to stay on task.*

Benny's tears disappeared, his smile making me want to slap his snout. ***Should I mention how you miss Rosanna's boobs and legs specifically?***

Benny!

His grin widened. ***Don't worry, I won't tell her your secret thoughts.***

Silence drifted by as I ignored him, the peach-and-lilac colored clouds causing the adrenaline to ease.

"I'm sorry," Gwenyth whispered, leaning further into me, "thank you for... for saving me..." Her eyes drifted closed as her breathing grew heavy.

A small smile formed on her lips, and I found I wasn't staring at the clouds anymore.

Rosanna can meet us in the next hour, Benny chimed in, ***looks like we're all fairly close to the same village.***

Alright then, I took a shaky breath, *let's go see Rosanna.*

3

———

HER SPECIAL POWER IS THINKING DICKS ARE DISGUSTING

GREEN ALGAE COVERED the dark stone walls behind the massive ogre in front of me. My muscles tensed: a large axehead made of black iron sat mounted on the wall, a high-pitched scream echoed throughout the room, and a bead of sweat dripped down my temple. The ogre narrowed his eyes.

With plans to meet my rival, Rosanna, and exhaustion from saving the princess pulling at my muscles, I knew I needed this. But first, I had to make a choice, and it had to be now.

The ogre cracked a knuckle. Then another.

Fuck. I'd run out of time.

"Alright, ok," I finally said. "I'll go ahead and take a double white mocha, extra whip and extra sweet. And, a dark coffee with four shots of espresso. Gwenyth?"

I turned to the princess who was having a spritely conversation with a gnome wearing purple-and-blue overalls.

"*Gwenyth.*"

"No need to yell," she said, turning, cheeks rosy. "I'll take the special. I think it's called," she squinted her eyes at the wood menu, "the Velvet-Wrapped Steel?"

"Fantastic," I grumbled, "alright, and a Velvet-Wrapped Steel."

"What size?" the ogre growled. "We have king, queen, or squire size."

"I'll take a king size!" Gwenyth said.

"We'll do king sizes for all of them."

We returned to the village's amphitheater where Benny had, of course, convinced the owner into letting him sing his newest songs to the fae folk suntanning in the flowery meadow. They had a generously-sized amphitheater, just big enough for Benny to curl up and swish his tail to his melody.

> *Ho Hey, slay the male fae*
> *Slash in the ass*
> *The gray-moralled prey*
> *Chomp off their heads*
> *Till they're well good and deads*
> *The morally-gray male-fae fillet*

Everyone cheered, more than likely thinking it was some folklore metaphor instead of a real event that *just* happened. It didn't seem to bother Gwenyth either, the terror from earlier having faded away from her face, leaving a gentle smile. A knot in my stomach unwound at the sight.

Even I couldn't stop a small grin from slipping along my mouth as I took in Benny's shining gold scales. Dragons rarely talked to any beings beside their dragon riders. Why would they?

But Benny was an exception. He loved meeting new beings, learning their stories, and getting to become friends. In all transparency, it inspired me from time to time.

I held up his drink and his pupils dilated.

Rhema! Benny spoke into my mind. *A post-performance treat? You shouldn't have!*

Don't make me regret it.

We maneuvered our way to the stage. He took the king-sized cup in between his square-cut talons and tossed the entire thing into his mouth.

Mmmm, nothing better than a red eye, he blinked at us. **Get it? Because I have red eyes?**

It gets funnier every time, bud, I replied, taking a sip of the sweet white mocha, savoring the whipped cream melting on my tongue.

Just what I needed.

Any creepy fae men lurking around for Gwenyth?

Not a peep!

Good. So where's Rosanna at? I asked. *It's been over an hour since her dragon told you they'd get here.*

Oh look at you, all flustered and excited to see her!

Not flustered—frustrated.

Is that what the humans are calling it nowadays?

Shut up.

Make me.

Benny, if I had a real choice in this matter, we wouldn't be seeing her until the annual guild reunion, alright? So why don't you calm down and tell me where they're at.

Benny held up a talon. **I believe that should be them right now.**

A screech peeled in the distance.

Gwenyth grabbed my arm. Before I had time to process *that* new development, a shout roared above us.

Large iridescent wings beat in the air, but it wasn't a dragon. Instead, it was a giant creature that looked more like a monstrous drago*nfly*: narrow blue body with round yellow eyes bulging out of its head. Sharp teeth were exposed to the air, but it was the woman with black braided hair and dark-brown skin choking the creature's neck with a sword that had me drop my king-sized double-sweet white mocha.

Grabbing Gwenyth's arm and running, I yelled at Benny to get out of the way. He darted into the sky, cheering Rosanna's name while she pierced the creature in its head with her second sword.

Rosanna and the fae monster landed on the amphitheater stage with a tremoring thud. Flowers and pollen scattered in the air, the fae folk shrieking as they ran towards the main village streets.

Gwenyth threw herself around my neck, and to be honest, I couldn't hear her screams anymore. All I could see, hear, and feel was Rosanna's warm laughter as she whipped her head back. Those long, thin braids arced through the array of pink flowers, her white smile shining as bright as the single sunbeam spotlighting her on the stage. Blood coated Rosanna's exposed shoulders and elbows, and her black-and-gold leather bracers.

Her godsdamn leather halter armor revealed the most tasteful amount of side boob—whoever her tailor was knew what they were doing—and her thigh-high boots blended into her skintight leather pants seamlessly.

Shit. Keep it together.

Sure, Rhemy, you definitely want nothing to do with her, Benny giggled.

Can you just get out of my head? I replied.

Then stop shouting your salacious thoughts at me!

I ignored him and the shiver running down my spine.

Sheathing her two swords into her scabbards, Rosanna stood up, hands on her hips. She cocked her head, rolling the creature underneath her boot.

"Almost feel sorry for the bugger, but I think gnomes deserve to keep their heads on their shoulders, don't you think, Idhynth?"

A green-scaled dragon descended on the empty meadow

with barely a sound. Her yellow eyes surveyed the area, locking on me. A broad smile widened on her mouth.

Whatever she said to Rosanna made her laugh again. Probably something about how clever they'd been last year when they swiped the last monster bounty hunter spot right from underneath Benny and me. One of our monster hunters had retired, opening the coveted spot, and Rosanna had known I was vying for that position.

She knew and took it anyway, and that—the hurt—is what I hated most of all, because I shouldn't have felt a thing.

I didn't *do* that anymore.

Rosanna turned, pinning me down with the same gaze that had resulted in me dropping my pants last year. I cursed at the way my heart beat hard and fast in my chest despite the boiling hatred in my belly.

Come on Rhemy, chin up! Shoulders down! You look like a frightened bird, not a sexy, intimidating warrior!

Not helping.

"Rhem," Rosanna shouted, jumping off the stage, "sorry we're late, had a bit of a run-in with a cursed dragonfly species. Far deadlier than we'd given them credit."

Her dragon, Idhynth, snorted in agreement.

"Looks like you took care of things, albeit you almost took out some villagers along the way," I gritted through my teeth, trying to wrench Gwenyth off of me.

"Glad you were there to herd them away," she smiled.

Gods, I wanted to punch her.

"New friend?" Rosanna asked, motioning to the princess who'd turned into a whimpering cat.

"Not exactly. This—" I grunted, peeling the shaking princess off me, "this is Gwenyth, Princess of the Southern Kingdom."

"And an unlucky victim of a predatory fae man, I'm guessing?"

Did she really have to say it like she didn't fucking know that already? As if she wasn't the reason I was in this position in the first place?

Her smug smile doused any attraction that'd been burning in my blood.

"If I'm a victim of anyone, it's Rhema." Gwenyth stepped forward.

Rosanna laughed. I rolled my eyes.

"So what," Gwenyth continued, "do you kill people's fiancés as well?"

Placing a hand on her hip, Rosanna flexed her veiny muscles. "Idhynth and I are more of the big-ferocious-monster-bounty type. Specifically in lakes and ponds, which this realm has more than enough of to go around."

"Ah," Gwenyth replied, "so you kill *real* monsters. How refreshing."

Red-hot jealousy flooded my mouth, every stinging word I wanted to tell Rosanna sitting on the back of my tongue. I bit them down.

"I wouldn't discount immortal men so quickly. Rhema's bounties are often far more tricky," she winked at me, "she's got a gift for identifying monsters with beautiful faces."

I gave her a wide smile, staring from her thigh-high boots up to her bare shoulders. "That I do, Rosanna."

Rhema, Benny retorted.

Rosanna's grin faded. She opened her mouth to say something, but stopped.

Typical.

"So what, does Rhema have some special power or something?" Gwenyth asked.

Before I could lash another insult at Rosanna, Benny interrupted with his high-pitched whine connecting all our mental bridges together as he said, *If her special power is thinking dicks are disgusting, then yes!*

I let out a loud groan. He wanted to change the subject, and I was too tired to fight against it.

"And that's because they're objectively gross." I replied. "I don't know how any of you can stand the sight of them, let alone... oh gods, nevermind. Rosanna, we need some help from a fae realm... expert."

Even saying that word made me want to grind my teeth.

Rosanna raised a brow. "What's going on?"

"I'd rather talk about it in private. Don't need any villagers to overhear and start spreading rumors."

Benny hummed a romantic tune into my mental bridge.

Rosanna replied, "There's a grove just on the other side of the village. It's said to be cursed, so no one goes there. We can have Idhynth or Benny connect our mental bridges and converse while they stay here and watch Gwenyth."

The heat from Rosanna's gaze caught me by surprise. My hands suddenly grew clammy and my chest tightened. Anticipation welled in my core as she parted her lips. Despite myself, I couldn't stop staring at the scar on her mouth.

Focus, Rhema, dammit. Don't give in to her and don't back down.

"Hold on, I want to go with you two," Gwenyth said.

"Princess," I replied, "just sit here and enjoy your king-sized Velvet-Wrapped-Steel, alright? This is bounty hunter business."

"And it involves *my* wellbeing. I should be a part of it."

Want me to cause a distraction? You can reward me with the best wingman award by getting me butter after this.

I don't want a wingman, Benny. We need answers.

And Gwenyth was right. This whole endeavor was for *her* safety.

"The princess should join us," I said.

Rosanna's throat bobbed, the heat in her gaze subsiding.

Thank gods.

I think.

"Then I guess we should all head to the grove. The villagers will think we're ridding them of the curse, so there shouldn't be any questions."

Rolling my shoulders back, I gave a nod. "Lead the way."

4

WHY ARE ALL THESE MEN WANTING TO MATE ME?

THE GROVE WAS COVERED in flowers and vines. Pink-and-purple blooms were scattered throughout the grass, and sunshine filtered in through the bright-green leaves. A group of goats meandered through the clearing, their orange eyes seeming to twitch.

I made a special effort to avoid them.

What's so cursed about this grove? It has such precious little goats! Benny spoke into all our minds.

I was thinking he looked tasty, Rosanna's dragon, Idhynth, growled back.

Idhynth, were you not there during the Equity for All Mammals meeting last month? Goats are considered a protected species now! No eating allowed.

A goat snorted and fell on its back with a thud.

I'd give it a painless, easy death, Idhynth continued, *and he looks salty...*

Idyhnth, down, Rosanna said, her tone steady and commanding, *we'll get you some rabbits later from your favorite farm.*

Idynth huffed a breath. *As long as I can get ten instead of five this time.*

Anything for my girl.

See Rhema, Benny said, *look how nice Rosanna is to Idhynth. You could learn a thing or two.*

I shook my head. *Last time I gave into your hungry pleads you over-ate and puked all over me, and I will not be dealing with that again. But I'm fine if Rosanna wants to indulge herself.*

Benny snorted. Rosanna and Idyhth shot me a glaring look. I grinned.

"Can we get to the point?" Gwenyth said. "Why are all these men wanting to mate me?"

She poked incessantly at my pauldron; I batted her away.

I filled in Rosanna and Idhynth on everything that had happened at Gwenyth's wedding: the fae prince talking about getting "let out by a warden" and "not letting luck like that pass him by". Gwenyth told them about the winged fae men who all claimed she was their mate and tried to steal her away at the lake earlier that day.

And they were all very sexy, Rosanna. I feel like I need to emphasize that since Rhema won't, Benny added.

Rosanna chuckled. "I always appreciate your thoroughness, Benny. It's actually very important to this case."

Benny hummed a spritely tune.

I raised a brow. "Is it?"

Rosanna nodded. "Did these men happen to be wearing all-black clothes with deep buttoned down "v"s and rolled-up sleeves?"

"Yes." I patted Gwenyth on the head who quickly swiped my hand away. "Why does that matter?"

"It's the CJM's uniform. Have you never heard of them before?" she questioned.

Simmering anger burned in my chest. "Should I have?"

"No, no, I'm not trying to—look, CJM stands for Chiseled-

Jawed Men, a term coined by fae realm locals for the fae men who attend the Enchantress' academy."

I looked at Benny. He shrugged.

"Could you be less cryptic? What academy? What Enchantress?" I asked.

"Ok, well, it's an academic program promising to help fae men find their one true love, which is extremely important in their culture. Apparently the Enchantress opened the program many centuries ago; some say it's as old as time itself. It's not uncommon to meet some CJM out here, but the way you're describing them is concerning. They're mostly known for being well-mannered and, if anything, are excessively polite."

I crossed my arms and tapped my foot. "CJM stands for 'Chiseled-Jawed Men'? Why wouldn't we—of all hunters—ever have heard of these immortal fae men before? Do you think we're idiots or something?"

"Gods, is Rhem more fiery than usual today?" Rosanna asked.

Yes! Finally, someone says it. Benny said.

"Maybe we should get her another one of those white mochas she loves? Whipped cream always seems to calm her down." She winked.

"It does?" Gwenyth questioned.

Great idea!

"Can we all focus here?" I groaned. "Besides, you've all got it wrong. It's not the whipped cream I like, it's the way the chocolate settles at the bottom so then I can scoop it out with a spoon at the end."

Everyone's eyes widened. My face heated.

"But that's not the point!" I seethed. "We have an actual issue on our hands."

Rosanna shook her head. "Look, I'm shocked too. I'd assumed you'd dealt with them before."

I couldn't deny the honesty in her face.

Well, now that we do know, I can tell you right now they were quite rude to our Gwenyth here, Benny interjected. *Tell 'em, Gwen.*

"They were nice at first," Gwenyth replied, her cheeks turning a flushed pink, "very nice, actually."

"Do us a favor and save us the details," I begged her.

She furrowed her brow. "But Rhema threatened lives and they became volatile."

"Not my fault they abducted her," I said.

I glanced up; Rosanna's eyes locked on mine, a gentle warmth in her smile, that familiar scar pulling down on her lip. Dammit. I swear, sometimes staring at her just felt like—

So anyways, Benny interrupted my thoughts, *since we know who they are now, how are we supposed to stop them? Just kill them?*

Rosanna stood up and paced around the grove, the twitching little goat following her steps. Gwenyth turned to me and gave a quizzical look.

Why was she staring at me like that?

"You'll need to see the Enchantress," Rosanna finally said, "it's obvious something went wrong, and this could cause problems for the whole realm, not just Gwenyth."

"Great," I grumbled, "this Enchantress better be just down the street."

Rosanna thinned her mouth. "She's a three days journey from here."

Three days? Benny and I shouted.

That means we're going to miss the first half of the Butter and Barmaids Festival, Benny whined, *and Rhema's been a cheapskate and won't buy me more butter balls unless we get them at the festival in bulk!*

"Benny's right, we don't have the time," I said.

"Idhynth and I would help, but we're drowning in bounties right now. And if these CJM's behaviors hold true, then they're going to keep going after Gwenyth as long as they think she's their mate."

The princess gulped. Our gazes met.

Despite the inconvenience she'd become these last few days, it'd been fucking terrifying watching how those CJM had tried to take her.

Festival or not, Rosanna being a bitch or not, Benny and I had a bounty job on our hands.

And we took pride in the quality of our work.

...It definitely had nothing to do with the fact that we didn't have the coin to get tickets for the festival without completing the bounty.

"Well, Princess, I suppose we're going to the Enchantress to figure out whatever the hell is happening," I said.

Gwenyth's usual spitfire attitude was completely gone as she gave a nod.

"I'm just... I'm taking in a lot right now." She looked like she was about to puke. "I need to use the latrine."

Normally I'd stick by her side, but she shoved me away. Benny, Idhynth, and the goats escorted her to a different part of the grove. The sounds of her retching echoed in the distance.

And by some stroke of awful luck, Rosanna and I were in the grove together.

Alone.

Well, almost alone.

This might take a while, Benny whispered as he and Idhynth left our mental bridges.

A bloated silence suddenly made me feel like *I* was the one going to puke.

"Well, since we have some time," Rosanna stepped towards me, "are you going to tell me what it feels like to stare into my eyes, Rhem?"

"What?" I laughed, an unbidden bead of sweat dripping down my face. "Sorry, you must have me confused."

"You've always struggled with keeping your thoughts in your own mental bridge."

Oh fuck me. That's why Benny had interrupted my thoughts earlier. She'd heard all of that—Gwenyth too.

Her smile widened even further, her scar stretching along her mouth. "I forgot how cute you get when you're all flustered."

My ears burst into flames. "Flustered? Look, once this bounty is done and the princess is returned home, I'll be able to enjoy some solitude at the Festival and that's all I care about."

"The princess, hm? I didn't take you for liking the dainty type?"

Rosanna closed the gap between us, her eyes searching my face, causing the warmth in my ears to drain into my cheeks.

"Me? And the—the princess? Oh gods, fuck no, not like that."

She stepped closer.

This wasn't going like it should; a buzz was in the air, like the night we fucked before she betrayed me the next day. And dammit, she smelled like cardamom and leather and oh gods, how I missed that smell. And the soft skin of her neck. And the rough scars on her arms. And the slender curve of her tits.

"Rhem," she whispered, taking another step towards me, brushing a loose strand of hair behind my ear.

I should punch her square in the jaw. Instead, here I was, the one melting like a godsdamn scoop of frozen cream on a hot summer's day.

"It's alright if you're into the princess," she continued. "I won't tell the guild. After all, you should be able to indulge in some rewards for all the dicks you have to deal with, right?"

My mind was swirling in various directions, sweat burning my skin.

"I take my bounty jobs seriously, Rosanna," I whispered,

packing heat behind my words, "something you should consider doing every once in a while."

She laughed, her breath brushing along my forehead. The few inches she had on me was overwhelming this close.

"How's that, Rhem?"

Bark scratched into my back. Had I been walking backwards? This wasn't good, I needed to get away from this woman. But I couldn't back down, either.

"You nearly killed civilians with that gaudy display earlier," I growled, "you need to be more careful. Take precautions. I can only imagine how many innocents have died at your hands amidst your bounties."

Running a single finger down my face, her smile softened. I flinched, but it wasn't from disgust like it should've been. It was from her warm calloused finger—the tip of her nail lightly scratching my cheek.

Just how I liked it.

"How many people have you killed in your time as a hunter?" she whispered.

I hesitated. Her eyes darted to my mouth, which was currently gaping like a fish because I'd given her bait and, like an idiot, I'd hooked myself on it. Too distracted by her little *show*.

"A few," I whispered.

"Translation:" she paused, leaning a hand on the tree, caging me in, and craning her neck down so her breath brushed my ear, "too many to count."

I couldn't refute facts.

"Hm," her lips brushed my ear. My eyes fluttered shut in response. The bark painfully bit into my hands, my grip the only thing preventing me from grabbing her waist. "It's impressive, you know. Killing people. It's something I admire about you. Does Princess Gwenyth like that part of you, too?"

"Fuck you," I breathed.

Rosanna smirked. "Just tell me when and where."

No. This was going too far. Not only had she stolen my chance at monster bounties, but she was trying to play me like some kind of toy she could wind up with sultry words and soft touches. She wanted something, but I wasn't going to give it to her this time—whatever it was—no matter how much I wanted to believe she was being sincere. I'd learned my lesson, and more importantly, I'd learned I wouldn't let her have a piece of me to hurt this time.

Yet that godsdamn cardamom-and-leather smell had me plastered to the tree, my hand obeying my wants instead of my needs as I reached to grab her tight leather pants—

A nearby tree rustled and all the heat in my face was replaced with a chill so cold I swear iced water had been thrown over us.

"Oh," Gwenyth gasped. "Oh, I'm so sor—"

Pushing off the tree, I shoved Rosanna away. Laughing, she stumbled back, a single braid framing her face.

"You're about as good at receiving compliments as ever." Rosanna flashed the princess a wink. "Take care of her, will you?"

Gwenyth stared at Rosanna in what was either awe or terror.

"We got what we needed from you," I spat at Rosanna, standing in front of Gwenyth, "go slay a crustacean creature or something."

Offering a salute, she said, "Will do. Good luck with those CJM."

She must've called for Idhynth in her mind because the dragon emerged over the treetops, slowly alighting onto the forest floor, allowing Rosanna to swing onto her back.

As they left, Gwenyth let out a loud breath. "She's really something."

Lost in the heat from it all, I replied, "She really is."

The princess stared at me with a question in her eyes, but before I could take back what I'd just said, Benny crashed through the trees.

Rhema, Gwenyth, I figured out why this place is cursed! he shouted.

I sighed. *Benny, myths and legends can wait, alright? Let's just head over to the Enchantress and get this done with.*

But it's the goats! They're actually—

Benny, I groaned.

Giving me a narrowed gaze, he offered his back to Gwenyth and I.

Suit yourself, he drawled.

I will.

Ugh, you're no fun sometimes, you know that?

Ignoring him, we ascended into the air and flew in the opposite direction of Rosanna: towards the Enchantress' academy for fae men.

5

AN UNNATURALLY GIRTHY MEMBER

THE FLIGHT TO THE ENCHANTRESS' domain was wet and miserable. Rain spilled from dark clouds like cold icicles, and because we were almost at our destination, Benny swore he couldn't fly any higher. I'd covered Gwenyth's ripped wedding dress with an extra cloak of mine, but it didn't stop the rain from seeping through the material, the princess shivering uncontrollably in my arms.

To top it all off, Benny was getting on my very last nerve.

Yes, even *more* than usual.

I still don't understand why you dislike Rosanna so much.

I gripped his leather reins tight, Gwenyth's slippery hands holding onto my forearms.

Benny, we have a job to do. Let's stay focused, otherwise we won't make it to the Festival at all.

Benny snorted and dipped into a thick cloud. Water drenched my face, hair, and leathers.

What the hells was that for? I sputtered, flicking the moisture off.

I need you to listen! Rhemy, how was Rosanna supposed to know you wanted the monster bounty jobs if you didn't even tell

her? Is she supposed to read your mind or something? Because I swear, if I wasn't able to do that, I'd have no idea what you could possibly be thinking most of the time.

Digging my heels harder into the stirrups, I leaned forward into the harsh movements of strong winds and Benny's wings.

She knew I wanted that job, Benny, I'd told her multiple times. So of course she knew what she was doing. And it was obvious I was tired of going after these dumb immortal men.

Just because you wanted that job didn't mean she didn't want it either. Besides, we're the only hunters in the immortal quadrant. Do you really think they would've let us move to the monster quadrant?

Molten anger rose into my throat. *Look, you don't get it, so I'm done talking about this.*

You know it probably means something that this meant so much to you, right? And I'm not talking about the monster bounties. I'm talking about how Rosanna hurt you.

Trying my best to block the rain from mine and Gwenyth's eyes, I said, *What's your point, Benny?*

It hurts so bad because you have feelings for her!

Clenching my jaw, I strained my thigh muscles. Rain ricocheted off of Benny's hard dragon scales and hit me instead.

The more I considered his words, the more I hated the truth in them.

You could be happy, Rhemy, I saw it last year when you and Rosanna were hitting it off! All you need to do is accept we're the best bounty hunters for immortal men, forgive Rosanna, and then you two can live happily ever after.

First of all, you can't tell me when I'm not happy, alright? Second of all, we were never happy. All we ever did was—

Fuck. Yeah, yeah, save me the gross details. But it's more than that and you know it. So what you need to do now—

Benny.

...is a grand gesture! We can turn back, go get her a big bouquet

of flowers or whatever it is you bounty hunters like—maybe a skewered goblin on a stick?—and you can apologize for being such an asshole—

Benny.

...and then you can confess all those feelings I know you keep deep, deep down. And if you just tell her the truth—

BENNY.

Then you'll finally be happy and let go of Emmaline—

BENNY, SHUT UP.

Benny's wings faltered and I lurched forward, biting down on my tongue.

A well of heat rose from my stomach and into my throat, memories from years ago welling up to the surface—memories meant to be locked away and burned: The war-torn villages, the nightly raids for resources, and the homecoming where I learned the nature of my wife's—Emmaline's—death, complete with the funeral I'd missed.

Two years of deployment, and in those final three weeks, I hadn't the faintest clue my world had ended.

I'd left and became a bounty hunter a week later.

Rhema, I just want to help, Benny said.

Well, don't.

But if you just tried, maybe you could have an actual life outside of this job!

Gwenyth was looking at me with big confused eyes, her mental bridge not having been connected to mine and Benny's. Looking down, my knuckles were white and I was holding onto her so tight she must've been in pain.

I tried to loosen my grip, but all I could see was Emmaline's face reflected in Gwenyth's: the faint firelight of our hearth dancing along her high cheekbones; her sweet smile gracing her lips whenever she read her favorite poems to me.

It hurt—this pain in my chest. I could handle blows and cuts to my body from battle, but this?

Something deep inside twisted and snapped.

You know what, Benny? Maybe if you weren't singing your stupid songs all day long, or going to get your talons manicured into useless shapes, or babbling about forest conservation with dragons who don't actually give a SHIT about saving trees, then we'd actually finish our jobs on time and I'd have a fucking life outside of the one I have with you. And then, maybe—just maybe—I might actually be happy for once.

Benny veered a harsh left. Gwenyth gripped my arms.

Oh yeah? he replied. **Well, you're just jealous because I actually make an effort with the beings I care about, whereas you have to be so upset at everyone all the time to make sure we're all just as miserable as you!**

Wind hitting my face to the point of pain, I laughed hard as I slapped his diamond-hard scales.

Me? Miserable? Benny, I'm the happiest, most light-hearted person I've ever met. However, when I have to look after not just a snot-nose diva, but Gwenyth too, then yeah, I guess my life does get pretty fucking miserable.

Benny jolted up through another heavy cloud, this time soaking Gwenyth and me to the point that she screamed.

Why are you so, so mean? Benny yelled.

Suddenly, his mental wall shut into place.

"Oh, we're not done with this," I shouted into the rain clouds.

I slammed against his mental bridge. It didn't budge.

"Real mature for an ancient creature! Can't handle a little argument without getting your feelings hurt, huh? Well, fine. I don't want to talk to you anyways."

Nothing but the sound of rain slapped against my face.

Guilt ran along my insides. Rarely was Benny the one to barricade our mental connection, and rarely was I this harsh with him. Yet hearing Emmaline's name...

...it was too much.

A lump sat in my throat and my lip started to tremble. Curling my fingers into fists, I willed the tears to stay behind my eyes, because they had to. They *had* to. I wasn't going to break, I refused to fucking break.

Arms wrapped around my neck and pulled me close. Everything stilled, surprise lighting my chest at how fierce Gwenyth held me.

"Everything's going to be alright," Gwenyth said into my ear.

Trembling more, I thought about grabbing her back and letting the tears roll out of me and onto her neck to mingle with the rain.

No.

I wouldn't break.

"That's sweet, Princess, but you can get off of me now," I replied. "Benny's just being an asshole, that's all."

Right, that's what was happening. Benny was being his typical, overbearing self and I was trying to make it through another day. All we needed to do was get Gwenyth home and make it to the Butter and Barmaids Festival—even if it was only for a few days instead of the full week. And if Benny and I weren't on speaking terms during it, so be it.

"It seems like there's more to it than that," Gwenyth replied.

"Trust me, Benny's just being a—"

Before I could finish, my stomach leapt into my throat as Benny nose-dived. Cursing every word I could think of, I held onto Gwenyth and the reins, her wet arms clutched around my neck as she shrieked.

Ears popping, we soared into a field surrounded by poplar trees. I rapped again on Benny's mental wall, but he didn't respond. Instead, we landed with a loud crack, and he bucked us off.

"What the hells?" I shouted, catching Gwenyth.

"He said he can't fly any further due to an enchantment," Gwenyth said.

Flaring my nostrils, I shook my head at him. "Seriously? You're going to use Gwenyth as your little mouthpiece? How childish can you get?"

"You can't hear him?" Gwenyth questioned.

"No, Princess, I can't. So what's the asshole telling you now?"

"He didn't say anything."

I smiled, spreading my arms wide as Benny glared at me with narrowed red eyes. "Fantastic. Well, lead the way Benny, and please let us know if there's anything you need from us. Food, water, praise for all your efforts—just say the word."

Gwenyth covered her mouth. "I'm not going to repeat what he just said."

"Fine by me," I grumbled. "If Benny wants to tell me something, he can say it to me himself. You don't need to let him bully you like this."

Gwenyth placed a hand on her hip. "You think I want to get caught between your lover's spat?"

A deep growling voice echoed through the trees. Stepping out of the shadows, a fae man with a sharp jaw and tall stature revealed himself. And, wouldn't ya know it, he was stark naked.

"Gwenyth, darling, there you are," he purred. "I've been looking for you."

"Good gods, more of you?" she yelled.

The fae man sprinted for Gwenyth—*fast*—his unnaturally girthy and huge member bouncing up and down.

That had to be painful, right?

"Can you just leave us alone?" I unsheathed my axe.

The fae male's eyes widened, but before he could retreat, my axe flew, followed by a stream of fire. My weapon landed right between his eyes while the fire scorched him into a pile of ash—along with my axe.

I stilled.

"My axe," I breathed, the hilt melting into a puddle before my eyes.

Crunchy grass bent underneath my knees as I tried to grab it, but the heat was too intense.

I looked up at my dragon who gave me a smug look.

"That's *it*," I whispered.

Rummaging into my trousers, I took out my enchanted cold pouch—the one I purchased from the Butter and Barmaids Festival years ago—and held it over the ashened corpse.

Benny's eyes darkened.

"Uh, Rhema?" Gwenyth said, "Why does Benny's voice suddenly sound deep and menacing?"

I smiled. "Because he thinks I won't do it."

But I would. Oh boy, *I would.* So I watched his little heart break into two as I dumped the last remaining butter balls onto the disgusting ashened fae man's flesh—right where his huge fat dick had been.

Eery silence filled the grove.

Then the earth shook, and Benny charged for me.

"*Stop!*"

Before I got pummelled by my two ton dragon, Gwenyth's 4'10" body stood between us, her head down and arms outstretched. Benny dug his heels into the dirt, lightly bumping her open palm with his snout.

"You two need to knock it off," Gwenyth said, looking between us.

Benny stuck out his tongue. I rolled my eyes.

"Benny, you stay outside and... and... come up with a new song or something," she instructed, whipping her damp hair across her shoulder. "Rhema, we'll go stay in that inn over there. They should have food, vacancy, and maybe even extra weapons for purchase."

"Did you hit your head or something?" I questioned, "There's no inn here."

She pointed behind me.

Sure enough, a quaint wood building with a smoking chimney sat between a dense grouping of poplar trees. Benny gave a loud snort and whipped around, his tail hitting my chest before he marched through a wide path of trees. I flipped him off.

"He says he saw that," Gwenyth muttered.

"*Good,*" I yelled.

"And he says he'll never forgive you for his butter balls."

"Tell him I don't care."

"He says—no, *no,* I'm done with this." She grabbed my arm and dragged me towards the inn.

I was too exhausted to resist.

INTROVERTS DON'T LIKE TALKING TO PEOPLE

THE TAVERN WAS WARM, the dim torchlight a sight for my sore, exhausted eyes. Gwenyth pushed me out of the rain and into the warm entrance, her dainty arms surprisingly strong.

I sighed. Fighting with Benny was never enjoyable, in fact, it always left me feeling like I was probably the worst person in all the realms. Benny's intentions were never out of malice. He was always trying to help everyone.

He was always trying to help *me*.

In truth, I knew I didn't deserve a dragon like him.

A small ding from the door brought me out of my thoughts. I inhaled the smell of baking bread and starchy soup like I was feasting on it already.

"What can I do for ya?" the barkeep asked us, his face sharp and angled, and his ears pointed.

"Two meals, two ales," Gwenyth turned to me, "and two waters. Plus we'll take two rooms."

"Excellent choices, although I'd highly recommend our nightly special: one bedroom with one bed for one gold piece. Great deal, if ya ask me," the barkeep replied.

"We'll pay extra for the two bedrooms," I said with a sigh.

"Ah, well, I'm afraid it's the only option available."

"Excuse me?" Gwenyth retorted. "No offense, but your place looks nearly deserted, surely—"

Before she could question him further, a couple walked down the rickety stairs.

"Excellent service as always, Bowen!" one of them exclaimed. "The perfect pit stop before the Butter and Barmaids Festival. Are you going this year?"

Dammit all to hell. If only we could leave tonight, then maybe I could make it on time and actually enjoy myself. Sit, relax, drink away these fucking feelings.

"Not this year, I'm afraid," the barkeep replied as the woman tossed him the key, "hope you enjoy it!"

The couple left without another word.

I leaned an arm on the wood bartop, "We'll go ahead and take that extra bedroom. Don't worry about the cleanup, we can manage."

The barkeep took the key and shut it in a drawer. "Sorry, Miss, only one bedroom with one bed."

I scoffed, leaning further across the bartop. "Let me say that again: we'll pay you for *two* rooms. That's double what you would get if we only took one room."

The barkeep leaned close, his voice down to a whisper. "Look, lady, I just work here, alright? Now will you take the damn special so we can move on with our night?"

Gwenyth scooted next to me. "Just give us the two rooms."

His mouth thinned. "It's against the Enchantress' law. Don't act like you don't know that."

"*What?*" I questioned. "What kind of law is that?"

"Do I look like I'm about to question her decrees? If I broke it and gave you two bedrooms, I'd be turned into a goat on the spot. Or maybe a pig."

"You're bluffing."

Suddenly, something solid rammed into my legs. A goat with orange eyes stared at me. It looked eerily similar to the ones back at the cursed grove where I almost gave into Rosanna's pursuits.

A chill ran down my spine.

"Let me introduce you to good 'ol Gilbert. He broke the one bedroom law three years ago, and now here he stands."

Gwenyth gulped. "On four legs."

Gilbert bleated, his wild eyes twitching.

"What the hell," I whispered.

So that's what Benny was trying to tell us about the herd of goats at the grove.

The barkeep continued, "But I will admit, he makes excellent milk for our residents."

Acid rose in my throat. Gwenyth gagged.

"So, the nightly special?" he asked.

"Fine," I conceded, "and what about the meals, are those only sold one at a time as well? Or will you turn into a spoon?"

"A spoon? That's a bit ridiculous, don't you think?"

Gwenyth and I shared a wary glance.

We ate our food first, and then headed up the creaking stairs. Thankfully, Gilbert only interrupted me once with a loud bleat while I was biting into some bread. Still, I swore his creepy little eyes could see through walls or something.

Stained walls and grimy floorboards met us as we entered the room, the mattress barely large enough to fit one person, let alone two.

"Guess I'll take the floor," I muttered.

"No," Gwenyth gripped my shoulder, a strange shiver running down my back at the gesture. "We can share."

The offer caused my chest to warm. I quickly doused it, hating the way I'd become so needy after our fiasco of a journey.

"Look at you," I replied, "a few days ago you would've slapped me for no reason, and now you're willing to share with a gross, greasy bounty hunter like me? I'm touched."

She furrowed her brow. "Why do you do that?"

I stiffened. "Do what?"

"Antagonize the shit out of people? Push them away?"

Shrugging out of her grasp, I hid the shock splitting into my bones. I hadn't been that obvious, had I?

I replied, "I'm what's called an introvert, Princess. We don't like talking to people."

"See, right there. What am I supposed to say to that?"

"If conversations with people are a struggle for you, I'm pretty sure you have royalty classes you can take to fix that."

Gwenyth stood inches from me, arms folded.

"Why did you make Benny upset?"

"*Me?*" I scoffed, "Gods, he's such a little..." I paused, leaning against the wall.

It wasn't Benny's fault, it was mine. And this princess wasn't going to let me get away with that excuse.

I sighed, "It's a long story, alright? Long, sad, and nothing that would interest you."

A small silence sat between us, something vulnerable in it. It felt thick, burdened, and I couldn't help but squirm.

"You're not as hard to figure out as you think," she muttered.

I scoffed. "Whatever helps you sleep at night."

Gwenyth shot me a glare. "Let me guess, you've got a tragic past, probably someone you deeply cared about died or left and you shoulder the blame for no godsdamn reason other than to not forget the pain. Because if you did, what would be left of them, right?"

My late wife's face flashed before my eyes. Happy, peaceful, and alive.

But she was dead.

Emmaline was fucking *dead*.

Unbidden fear flared through my muscles, hot and pulsing. Without thinking, I pushed Gwenyth against the wall and drew my dagger at her neck. She hitched a breath, her throat bobbing, the weapon's edge lightly scraping her skin.

"Talk to me like that again, and I'm letting those fae freaks abduct you once and for all."

"You couldn't even if you tried," she whispered.

Clenching my jaw, I leaned in so close her breath mingled with mine. "You really want to test me right now?"

Her gaze darted from my eyes to my mouth. "Benny said I don't have to be scared of you."

A retort sat on my tongue, but instead of spitting its poison, I swallowed it. Shoulders falling away from my ears, I hung my head. Even after telling him off, dumping the last of his butter balls, and being an all-around bitch to him, he saw through all my bullshit.

Despite seeing the worst parts of me over the years, Benny still saw me as *good*.

I kept my grip steady, readying to spill some blood and prove them both wrong—but what I didn't expect was how Gwenyth's gray eyes had flecks of green and gold in them.

"If I didn't know better, I'd say you like being pinned like this," I rasped.

Her smooth, delicate fingers wrapped around my wrist. Slowly, she lowered my dagger away from her throat, brushing her nose with mine. Anger gave way to something deeper— something primal.

"What if I do?" she teased.

Fingernails digging into my palms, I kept my hands from wrapping around that small waist of hers and pinning her against me.

Fuck. What was wrong with me? One moment I'm thinking Gwenyth looks like my dead wife, the next I'm thinking about what her tongue might feel like against mine?

She chewed her lip, and suddenly I couldn't remember why I'd threatened her in the first place.

"Are you and Rosanna... together?" she whispered.

My ears burned, taken aback by the sudden ask.

"No," I replied.

"Oh," she said with a furrowed brow, "are you certain?"

I didn't stop her as she traced my jaw with her finger, sliding it down my neck, a light scratch making my breaths grow heavy.

"We..." I gulped, "we fucked once, a while ago, but that's it."

"I see." Her eyes became quizzical.

I held a breath, my fingertips burning with need.

"I'll be marrying a prince when I return home, one I've never met before. The maids tell me he's well-mannered, fairly handsome, and will serve the kingdom well." She paused, pressing her palm against my chest. "I know you're hurting right now, and to be completely transparent, so am I. But if you're open to it, we could forget about those things together. Just for the night."

Head spinning, I told myself she was too innocent—she didn't know what she was asking for right now.

She giggled. "Gods, I'm kind of fucked up, aren't I?"

Laughter escaped my mouth, and I found myself leaning my chest against hers. I missed feeling close to someone, even if only for a single night. Benny had said I deserved to be happy—was that true?

Gods, way to be philosophical about all of this.

Whether I deserved happiness or not didn't matter. But fun? That was a better question. Fun was simple, not drowned in sadness, tears, and gut-wrenching memories.

I think we both deserved at least that much.

"I'm supposed to make sure you're taken care of," I whispered.

Her eyes brightened as she wetted her lips. This shouldn't

be happening; I was supposed to stay focused, return her home, and be done with it. Instead, here I was, basically on my knees for a woman who'd reminded me of a love I had once called mine.

Eyelids growing heavy, she stared at my mouth. "Then you better do it."

Any of my resistance had turned to ash, the fire billowing in my core turning relentless. I dropped my dagger. It clattered on the floor.

"*Fuck it,*" I whispered, mouth crashing onto hers.

She breathed me in with a desperate moan, her tongue taking no time to find mine. Fingers digging into her soft skin, I pulled her tight against my body, her heat seeping into me as she wrapped a leg around my torso.

Oh gods, she had me, didn't she? Since day one, she'd been figuring me out and I hadn't the faintest clue.

Not dumb, not desperate—Gwenyth was clever as hell. And something about that made me ravenous.

"Get on the bed and spread your legs for me," I demanded.

Eyes flitting to mine, her cheeks burned a bright red. She obeyed, lying on top of the sheets, her ripped wedding dress ruffled precariously high on her slender thighs. One of her straps was hanging off her shoulder, her nipples peaked against the thin material. Gods, she really was a small thing, and she was beautiful, too.

Pushing her legs further apart, I kneeled before her, sliding my hand up her leg.

"Is this what you wanted, Princess?" I whispered into her ear. "You want me to fuck you until you can't remember your own name? My hands on your pussy, my tongue savoring your taste?"

Gwenyth nodded, her breaths short and heavy.

I could feel the heat between her legs, the want radiating

from her body: release from worries, from the future, from duties.

Maybe I should've found some self-control in all of this, but I didn't want to. I wanted release from all the unbidden memories flooding me. And, to be fair, she owed me when she slapped me in the face for saving her, and I owed her for killing her fae prince fiancé.

Fair trade.

I nipped at her inner thighs, her muscles tensing and legs closing in on me. Adrenaline rushed through my body as she let out a soft moan.

Oh fuck.

I kissed up to her lower stomach, riding her dress to the swell of her tits and climbing on top of her; she shuddered as I pressed a kiss to her neck. She gripped my arm, a soft moan accompanying her tight grip when I trailed my hand over her full breasts and down to her center.

"So wet for me already, Princess?" I purred, nearly losing it.

She cried in my ear as I plunged a finger into her. And then I gave her a second, her grip tightening on my arm to the point of pain.

"Too much?" I asked.

She shook her head. "More."

I tsked. "You're so used to getting your way, aren't you?"

Her brows dipped, a curse sitting on her tongue as I edged her.

I smiled. "Beg, Princess. Beg, and I'll do it."

"*Please,*" she breathed. "*Please,* Rhema, I need you."

Something about hearing my name on her lips had me succumb quicker than I'd meant to.

"Much better," I replied.

Her whimpers and cries caused my own wetness to slip between my legs. I slid between her thighs, tossing her legs over my shoulders.

My name screamed out of her lips while I licked her center, the tanginess a rush to my own pleasure. I swirled my tongue just below that spot she needed, my gasped name confirmation.

But there was nothing more disappointing than an early release. Building up to it was the fun part, and this princess was going to break from her pleasure so beautifully.

Teasing, nipping, and sucking, her moans and cries grew desperate, her fingers pulling at my hair while my hands wandered to her tits, pinching and causing her to writhe against my tongue.

And I couldn't fucking stop myself.

She broke under my tongue and wandering hands. I held her thighs tight, not allowing her to retreat from me. Lick after lick and she pulsed in my grasp, sending heat into my core, my own moans escaping my lips.

And then I released her.

Thinking that was all she wanted, I meant to get up and take the floor, but instead she grabbed my tunic and pressed her mouth against mine. I caged her in, letting her taste herself on my tongue.

"My turn," she gasped.

I widened my eyes. "Are you sure about that, Princess?"

"Just do it, Bounty Hunter."

She didn't have to tell me twice. I rolled onto my back, allowing her to slide my pants off and toss them to the side. Her eyes looked hungry, and shock broke through my body when I finally saw it in her gaze:

This wasn't Gwenyth's first time with a woman.

Grabbing my thighs, she teased me just about as well as I teased her—kissing between my legs, slowly working her tongue over my center and circling so goddamn slow.

Fuuuuuck.

Gwenyth finally circled her tongue over my clit, and it took everything within me not to scream her name, Rosanna's name, *anyone's* name—

A talon rapped on my mental bridge as she sucked my clit into her mouth. *Dammit*, of all the times for Benny to request access, it would be now when my concentration was next to none.

My mental barrier shattered before I could stop it.

Rhema, he started, *I know it's been a few hours since we've talked, and I just wanted to say I'm sorry for shutting you out for so long.*

Well fuck, I couldn't get him out of my head now and of all the things he was doing, he was apologizing? While I was about to come?

It's—it's alright, Benny, I managed to say, *I'm the one who should be sorry. Let's—let's save this for the morning.*

But he didn't leave. *I just needed to tell you that while all I want for you is a good and happy life, I know that badgering about Rosanna wasn't the right thing to do.*

I was so fucking close.

Benny, can we talk about thi—

Another time? I would, but Rhemy, we haven't talked for an entire two hours! I even wrote a song for you that I wanted to sing to you, and I was even thinking— He paused. **Rhema, are you...?**

I groaned. *Yes!*

Benny strung a line of curses. **You couldn't keep it in your pants for one fucking day?**

Benny, out!

Ahhh, not again! Make it stop, make it stop, make it sto—

His mental barrier slammed shut again, but it was too late. Any ride towards pleasure in my body was gone.

Fantastic.

I gently instructed Gwenyth off me. She was so drunk with pleasure she didn't appear bothered by my early retreat; she even snored the moment her head hit the pillow. I couldn't help but laugh.

At least Benny and I were talking again.

And at least Gwenyth had some fun before going back to her duties. As did I.

Not that any of those things would necessarily help with figuring out this whole Enchantress-fae-men shit, but I'd argue they were important in their own ways.

7

YOU'LL BE CHARGED A SMALL HARASSMENT FEE

UNLIKE ME, the morning came quick.

The inn we stayed at thankfully had a forgery in the back with a forgemaster who worked at alarming speed. Within a few hours, I had a new axe that was lighter, shinier, and sexier.

The faes certainly knew how to make good-looking weapons.

Leaving Gwenyth to buy a new tunic dress from one of the shopkeepers, I walked with Benny to the forest's edge.

Benny, I started, letting out a long breath, *you know I can get… overwhelmed. Especially when talking about the monster boun-ties, Rosanna, Emmaline, or maybe more things than I care to admit.*

Benny's red eyes beamed. ***I know, Rhemy, and I shouldn't have pushed so hard about your feelings for Rosanna. Even after all these years, it makes sense Emmaline is still on your mind and that you'd rather not be with anyone right now.***

I know what you were trying to do and, in all honesty, I think I needed to hear it.

Aw, Rhemy, are you apologizing?

I-I'm…

A smile widened on his scaly mouth.

I slapped my hand over my face. *Benny, look, I'm sorry for my words. When I said if I had time away from you I'd finally be happy...*

He looked at me expectantly.

I didn't mean it. Doing bounty jobs with you, monsters or immortal men... it's made my life exciting. It's what I look forward to when I go to sleep and when I wake up.

And why's that, Rhemy-boo? Benny crooned.

Fluttering my eyes shut, I bit down on my cheek. There was only one way back into his good graces, and I wasn't going to let my apology fall flat after all this effort.

Because I love you, Benny-boo, I whispered.

What was that? Did you hear something? I think my mental bridge is acting up, Rhemy, you might have to say it out loud. In fact, I need you to yell it.

Gods. The things I do for him.

I opened my mouth and yelled at the top of my lungs, "Because I love you, Benny-boo."

Birds fluttered out of trees and into the blue sky. Benny cheered and whipped his tail on the ground in excitement.

Apology accepted! Can I hold your new axe now? It's so shiny, he drooled, his long tongue flopping out of his scaly mouth.

I sheathed it. *So you can melt it again? No thanks.*

I didn't mean to!

And yet it happened anyway.

Gwenyth interjected. *I thought you both were done fighting?*

Yeah, Rhema. And good friends let each other hold their deadly, pretty weapons. Especially when they drop all their butter balls on the ashes of a huge dick, Benny chided.

Touch my new weapon and I'll never buy you butter balls at the Festival again.

Benny bumped my arm with his snout. **You sicken me.**

All in a day's work. I patted his head.

And with that, we set off together for the Enchantress' keep to solve our fae-men-being-obsessed-with-Gwenyth problem.

A wood sign hung between two bright-green poplar trees and judging by its painting of a woman with a staff, we were headed in the right direction. The ground was beaten down by footprints, horseshoes, and other animal marks I couldn't recognize.

"Seems we aren't the only ones wanting to see the Enchantress," Gwenyth said, placing her hands in the pockets of her fresh tunic dress. It was pink and stitched with blue-and-green roses, hugging her curves in all the right places.

"I guess so," I replied a bit too breathlessly.

Who knew Rhemy would be into a princess? Benny smirked.

Benny, I swear to the gods—

I know, I know. No match-making, I got it. But I will say, she's got great book taste. She gave me some recommendations when you and I weren't talking yesterday, and she's quite the wild one.

That certainly explained a lot.

Magic stirred in the air, growing stronger the further we went, its smell and taste like overly-steeped tea.

It was then Benny started humming a tune that made the hairs on my neck stand.

Butter, butter, butter, oh the deliciously tasty stuff.

Smother it in stew, spread it on guts,

And so I'll sing until I can't get enough.

"Benny, did you not get enough breakfast this morning?" I asked carefully.

He bobbed his head as he continued walking beside me, his red eyes glinting brighter than I was comfortable with.

Not a lot of animals in these parts, he said into mine and Gwenyth's mental bridges, *I've only found a few bunnies since we got here last night.*

"We can take a break and find some more," I suggested, letting the sunshine hit the gleam of my new axe.

Oh I'm perfectly fine. No need to worry.

Benny, do I need to remind you what happened last time you didn't get enough food?

Benny averted his gaze as he picked up his pace. **That barkeep was a horrible person. Besides, he was going to die sooner or later.**

All people die sooner or later.

My point exactly.

This wasn't good.

Look, if you're going to go on a feeding rampage, at least eat the fae men who keep following us.

I would if they didn't taste so bland.

Dear gods. So he'd already tried one.

"Should we be worried?" Gwenyth whispered as she stepped next to me.

I tapped my axe's hilt. Benny wasn't at his full state of hunger yet, otherwise his red eyes would turn pitch black, but he was walking dangerously close to it. If he did go on a rampage, the only way to stop him was feeding him butter.

Which, thanks to me, we were all out of. Not that we had enough to start out with, anyways.

"Just let me know if you see any bunnies or rodents we could feed him," I replied.

The princess gulped.

We're here! Benny exclaimed.

Sure enough, a long line of people dressed in robes and pointy hats stood before us. And ahead of them, a huge shimmering wall, of what looked to be an enchanted barrier, fanned out as far as the eye could see.

"Hark!" a loud nasally voice called out, "Are you three here to attempt to solve the Enchantress' riddle?"

Gwenyth shrieked as a floating head trapped in a bubble approached, the head's jawline sharp and his black hair luscious.

"And what the fuck are you supposed to be?" I questioned.

"My name is Nathaniel, and I'm the keeper of her Enchantress' barrier. Are you here for the riddle?"

"We're here to see the Enchantress. We've got some personal complaints regarding her Chiseled-Jawed Men."

"Ah, I see," Nathaniel replied, "if the size is too girthy, we highly recommend our new and improved enchanted lubricant, *You Take Me So Well*. Going for a hot deal right now at only five gold coins."

He pointed to an old hag standing behind a lopsided wood table. She waved at us with an apple-shaped tube of whatever the fuck that lube was enchanted with.

Probably STDs.

Can I eat Nathaniel? Benny asked.

Maybe later, I replied.

Oh gods, Gwenyth groaned.

"That's not our issue," I told Nathaniel, "can we just speak to her? Privately?"

"If it's not a Code 55, then I'm afraid you'll still need to solve the riddle. No correct answer, no Enchantress."

"Is that what all these people are doing here?" I questioned, motioning to what I now realized were wizards and sorcerers, all of them holding huge stacks of ancient dusty grimoires.

"Indeed! They've traveled far and wide to try and solve the Enchantress' ancient riddle so they can witness the divine work of her academy so they, too, might find their one true love. But I must offer a fair warning—only fae men are able to get by because they're not required to answer the riddle. All the non-fae-men-folk we've encountered have failed."

As if on cue, an elderly man hobbled past us, tears streaming down his face.

"All my decades of studies—for nothing," he cried. "*A waste of a life!*"

He tore his robes apart, completely exposing himself. But,

his pointed hat remained. So many weird, naked men in the fae realm.

Gwenyth, shield your eyes, Benny placed his talons in front of her face.

Then the man ran down the path and out of sight.

"So if you could just wait in line for your turn…"

"How about we go now?" I asked, unsheathing my new axe and swiping it dangerously close to his bubble form.

Nathaniel shrieked. "I—no, no! You must wait in line."

I grinned. "Benny?"

Ooo! Eating time! He opened his massive jaws towards Nathaniel.

"Wait, wait! Alright, fine, you three are next." His iridescent eyes widened as he whooshed back. "Just follow me, and do not threaten anyone else here, understand Bounty Hunter? The Enchantress runs a respectable establishment!"

I smirked. "I'm sure she does." Turning to Benny I motioned for him to close his jaws.

He whined in protest. *So hungry, Rhemy.*

I know, I'm sorry bud. We'll see if the Enchantress has anything, alright?

Gwenyth rubbed Benny's neck as we followed Nathaniel to the front of the line. Wizards and sorcerers grumbled and heckled us, but one foul look from me and they all shut up.

Ah, I loved doing that.

A blaring cacophony of violins and lutes made me jump. Nathaniel's bubble popped. The magical barrier swayed and rippled as a sharply chiseled face appeared, the man's long flowing black hair framing his jaw perfectly.

It was Nathaniel. Again.

"There you are, travelers," Nathaniel said in a low growl, a stark contrast to his nasally voice, "we've been waiting for you."

I stepped forward, axe in hand. "Just give us the damn riddle already."

He stopped, furrowing his brow and letting out a harsh sigh. "Then let me do my job!"

Can I eat him now? Benny asked.

Not yet.

Butter, butter, butter, oh the deliciously tasty stuff.

Smother it in stew, spread it on guts,

And so I'll sing until I can't get enough.

Violins and lutes erupted again. Gwenyth stumbled into me. I held her waist, and I didn't miss her smell of fresh peonies—a scent that was starting to be familiar.

"There you are, travelers, we've been waiting for you," Nathaniel said again. "You've arrived at the Enchantress' keep, and you wish to enter. But no such privilege is easily given. For you, a single riddle must be solved within the hour, three guesses be your limit, and only if you utter the correct one might you walk into her graces and behold the Enchantress' beauty. For many a traveler we have had, wizards and scholars of greatest degree, and yet none have been able to decipher this sacred puzz—"

"Just get on with it," I yelled.

The floating head coughed again, voice nasally, "Now I have to start over."

Benny rose up on all fours, towering over everyone like a small castle. He roared so loud the ground shook and trees crashed to the ground. All the while, he sang in mine and Gwenyth's head:

Butter, butter, butter, oh the deliciously tasty stuff.

Smother it in stew, spread it on guts,

And so I'll sing until I can't get enough.

Gwenyth looked at me with wide eyes. Benny's muscles rippled, and his gaze flickered in between bright red and black.

Fuck.

"The riddle," I repeated, "now."

"Alright, alright, alright," Nathaniel coughed and rippled out of view, replaced by a fanciful script:

> *Liquid gold, yet clear as glass*
> *Upon the dagger which doth plunge deep*
> *Be not afraid of worthy mass*
> *Excite the sheath to pleasure reap.*

"Five gold coins!" the old hag yelled from behind. "It'll take the edge right off and slide him right in! Discount will be gone by tomorrow!"

And then, the answer hit me clear as day.

"Oh my gods," I whispered.

"What?" Gwenyth questioned. "Did you figure it out?"

Sliding my hand down my face, I nodded.

"Nathaniel," I called.

The floating head appeared, his iridescent eyes glistening. "If you wish to forfeit, it's no trouble at all. You'll just be charged a small harassment fee for how you treated me earlie—"

"Lube," I said.

Everyone fell quiet.

Nathaniel's face turned white. "Why, um, yes, you can buy some of the enchanted lube on your way out."

"No, dumbass. The answer to your fucking riddle is lube; it's literally spelled out with the first letter of each sentence. Now let us in."

"No way," Gwenyth snickered.

He guffawed, "What? No, no, that's—wait, no—"

Violins and lutes shattered my eardrums again as the riddle disappeared. Mouth agape, Nathaniel's eyes bulged out of his head. All the wizards and sorcerers erupted in angry shouts and heckling cheers.

"No one's solved it before," he gasped, "wait, let's make a

deal, hm? A trade? How about ten tubes of lube for free, and you can head back the way you came!"

"No thanks," I retorted, "now let us in."

"Trust me, it's boring in here, nothing to see," he said, ignoring me, "oh gods, wait, no, you can't come in—!"

But the magic shield cracked down the middle, all the way up to the sky. More music blared as it slowly parted for us like huge double doors. Beyond us was the Enchantress' castle, a sparkling jewel ladened with silver, sapphires, and rubies, tucked against a sprawling hill dotted with pink-and-orange flowers.

Alright, Benny, let's go ahead and find you some—

Butter! Benny cried.

Air pushed against us as he took off into the Enchantress' domain, his gold scales glittering against the sun, his fire flaming into the sky.

Oh no.

We ran after him, and to my dismay, Nathaniel reappeared as a floating bubble and followed us, yelling all kinds of different deals—I think I even heard him say an enchanted dildo with three dicks.

Who needed three dicks, let alone one?

Benny, I called into his mental bridge, *you have to calm down!*

Butter, butter, butter, oh the deliciously tasty stuff.

Listen to me!

Smother it in stew, spread it on guts,

And so I'll sing until I can't get enough.

"He's not stopping," Gwenyth cried.

We came to a stop at a bridge overlooking a massive lake sparkling like rainbows. Benny soared high above us, scorching his flames into the air.

"He's too far gone," I told Gwenyth. "The only way to solve this is to find butter and find it now."

But my thoughts were suddenly lost as a large black shadow covered the sun.

Not a shadow.

A horde of winged men.

"Your dragon is not welcomed here! Nor are any of you!" Nathaniel screamed from his little bubble.

But his nasally voice was quickly drowned out by the Chiseled-Jawed Men's rumbling shouts as they soared through the sky, directing their swords towards Benny and plummeting towards him with reckless abandon.

"And... they're all gonna die," I said.

Benny released a roar that pierced the sky. Power ricocheted through the air and into the ground, the force so intense my knees shook, causing us to crumple onto the sparkling marble bridge. Fire erupted again from Benny's jaws, the spray aimed at the entire swarm of men.

Every single one of them turned to ash.

"Oh my gods," Gwenyth shuddered.

Arbentaliathoxian, the most powerful dragon in the world. Funny how easy it was to forget that sometimes.

"Butter. *Now!*" I shouted.

Ignoring Nathaniel's annoying screeches, we rushed towards the castle, yelling in earnest for someone—anyone—to grab as much butter as they could find. Fae men with ethnically ambiguous skintones, warm smiles, and glimmering eyes rushed out to meet us. Some wore the CJM's uniform—all-black outfits with a precariously buttoned-down shirt and sleeves rolled up to their forearms—while others wore aprons, blacksmith overalls, and a few had princely attire.

"Your beauty doesn't even rival the stars, for what can outshine a diamond like yourself?" one of them yelled.

"What?" Gwenyth and I exclaimed.

"If this was all the time we had left, I wouldn't have traded it for anything," another man said.

"Someone please just use your brain and get us butter or we're all going to die," I yelled.

"In every lifetime, it was always you," another man proclaimed.

"For fuck's sake—"

"Butter, darling?" a fae man with black hair asked. He wore an apron with no shirt underneath. Holding a plate with ten sticks of butter piled on top of one another, he smiled.

"Finally, someone who listens. But we're going to need more than that. Can you manage that?"

He passed me the plate. "Anything for you, darling."

"Alright, calm down and let's get to work, twinkle toes. Gwenyth? I need you to stand in that field right there with this plate and get Benny's attention."

"But he's going to eat me," she cried.

"No, he won't. Once he smells the butter and sees it's you, he'll calm down. Just throw it in the air once he's close enough and you'll be fine. Now go. I need to keep these idiots focused."

Gwenyth slowly let go of my arm, her gray eyes steady as she took a deep breath. She offered a strong nod despite the way her lower lip trembled.

I rushed into the castle with the fae. Benny's roars continued to shake the grounds as we maneuvered through the kitchen's cold boxes. The guy was picking the butter sticks individually out of the box and placing them onto a shiny new plate like a fucking psychopath.

"Just carry the damn things," I instructed, picking up three of the five boxes.

"Of course, darling."

"Never say that again."

"Anything for y—"

"Shut up and let's go."

We made it out just in time. Benny had spotted Gwenyth who stood in the field with four fae men yelling gods knows what at her. But she didn't seem to notice them as she screamed, throwing the plate of butter in the air right as Benny flew downward.

He slurped up the sticks as if they were scraps. The black-haired fae man and I rushed out to join her, opening the cold boxes and throwing the butter at Benny. Purring like a giddy animal, Benny licked and slurped every last pound of butter, the glint in his black eyes returning to its normal sheen of red as he slumped to the grassy knoll with a thud.

I love butter, he said into my mental bridge.

Wiping the sweat off my face, I replied, *Yeah, I know.*

He gasped. *Did I do it again?*

Go on a killing spree and manage to destroy an entire army in one go? Yeah, you did.

Oh dear.

"Um, guys," Gwenyth interrupted us, "I think I found the Enchantress."

A woman clad in gold-and-green robes was running towards us, waving a staff in the air, yelling something about how we were trespassing on her property. A spiral of yellow light erupted from the staff she had pointed at Benny. Power burst from the tip, colliding with his stomach. The light fizzled with a pop.

"Where's Nathaniel?" I asked. "He needs to tell her we solved the riddle."

But the bubble man was gone.

And the Enchantress had decidedly changed her mind about Benny and was now pointing her staff at *me.*

Well, this should be fun.

8

NOTHING BETTER THAN FREE ENTERTAINMENT AND BUTTER

A RAY of power soared towards me. I sliced my axe at it, the fae steel catching the magic and deflecting it back towards the Enchantress. She dodged, the ray of power hitting one of the Chiseled-Jawed Men instead. The man flared into yellow light and reappeared as a frog. Gwenyth and I gasped.

Banging her staff with her hand, the Enchantress turned and pointed it at Gwenyth.

"Whoa, whoa, whoa," I jumped in front of the princess, hands raised, "hold on, we just came here to ask some questions."

"Questions?" the Enchantress yelled, "By the looks of it, you aren't here to chat, but to kill all my students! How the hells did you get in here?"

I furrowed my brow. "It's your precious students that brought us here in the first place."

"My students are excellent in all capacities," she replied, "and since you've clearly harmed Nathaniel in order to trespass my barrier, you must be turned into fish."

"We didn't trespass," Gwenyth argued, "we solved your riddle fair and square. Ask Nathaniel yourself!"

The Enchantress' brows raised so close to her hairline I thought they'd fly right off.

"Do not lie to me, child. Now hold still so I can transform you into a gross little hagfish."

Six fae men stepped in front of us, all of them yelling in unison, "I would die for her, even if it meant I couldn't live."

The Enchantress gasped, her eyes darting back and forth between the CJM like a wild fluttering bird. Then, her stare landed on Gwenyth again, but this time, her face softened.

"I see," she sighed, lowering her staff. "Men, remember our lesson on reiteration and logic? Just because you say something twice in a different way doesn't make it more romantic. It can even reduce its effect because you'll come across dumb."

One of the men raised his hand. "What should we have said instead, Enchantress?"

"Try, 'I would die for her, even if she didn't ask it of me.'"

All of them said some "ooo"s and "ahh"s, thanking the Enchantress and repeating the phrase back and forth to each other.

"What in the hells is happening?" Gwenyth whispered.

"No clue."

Isn't it obvious? Benny asked. *She's teaching them!*

"Precisely right," the Enchantress replied, hitting her staff on the ground with a clink, "your dragon's a sharp one, bounty hunter."

What a sweet woman.

She just threatened to turn us into fish, Benny.

Everyone has their flaws.

"And Gwenyth," the Enchantress continued, "you must be the princess that my students can't stop talking about. How obtuse of me. Well, I daresay I owe you an apology after threatening to turn you into such slippery creatures."

"So, you're not going to kill us?" I checked. "Even though Benny incinerated an entire horde of CJM?"

"If they were dumb enough to fight a dragon, then they were never going to graduate and find their true love. Better they get incinerated here than die out there of a broken heart."

Ouch. Harsh, Benny said. *And, to be fair, you also tried to kill me.*

"Ah, yes, well, suppose the apple doesn't fall far from the tree," she replied.

A fair assessment.

"Look," I said, "I don't understand whatever the hell is going on here, but we came because we have a major problem with your students, or CJM, or whatever you call these fae men."

Even as I said it, Gwenyth was shooing away the men surrounding us, each of them staring at her hair, face, eyes, and... other places. I unsheathed my axe and glared.

"Boys, *boys!*" The Enchantress shouted at them, "Away from her. Now."

Faces downtrodden, the fae men backed away, offering apologies as they returned to the castle.

"I'm terribly sorry, Gwenyth, my dear," the Enchantress continued, "you see, fae men are most drawn to young women who are in search of their one true love, of which your desire is greatest in all the land at the current moment."

Gwenyth's cheeks flushed. "I'm not *that* desperate."

"According to my students, you are."

"And that makes it ok for them to be hunting her down?" I interjected, pointing my axe at the magical woman. "Maybe you're our real issue, not these weird, sexy men."

"Maybe your prejudice towards the fae is the problem, Bounty Hunter."

Get ready for phase two, I said solely into Benny's mental bridge.

Aw, but I like her, Benny replied.

Enough to not protect Gwenyth?

Benny gasped. *You're right! No one touches our Gwenyth.*

Standing to his full height, Benny slammed down to the earth, digging his claws into the green grass, standing over Gwenyth and I as he growled so loud it shook the ground.

The Enchantress' face paled.

"Now, tell your students to stop stalking Gwenyth, or you're done here," I seethed.

"Alright, alright, let me explain." Placing her staff on the ground, she raised her hands. "I can't just 'call them off'. You see, these fae men come of their own accord to my academy when their desire to find their one true love forms in their hearts. They agree to stay here until graduation, only going on supervised excursions when appropriate with the curriculum. And while it's embarrassing to admit, we had an unprecedented breach three weeks ago. Hundreds of them left without a chaperone and... well..." she paused, scrunching her eyes, "they've been nearly impossible to find. I still don't know who let them out."

"A breach?" Gwenyth questioned. "Rhema, didn't my fae fiancé say something about being let out before you killed him?"

"He did," I replied. "He told us it was a warden of some kind."

"A warden?" the Enchantress questioned. "But I don't assign any students to be wardens..."

Her voice trailed off, and her eyes widened.

"Nathaniel!" she screamed.

A bubble appeared between us, inside of which was none other than the chiseled jaw and iridescent eyes of the headless riddle asshole who tried to sell us enchanted lubricant.

"Enchantress!" Nathaniel's feigned smile made my stomach queasy. "Oh, I'm so sorry, I must get back to the barrier at once. There's some sorcerers who are buying loads of that excellent new lubricant you made, and I'm hoping to sell out before they leave for the Butter and Barmaids Festiva—"

"Nathaniel, darling," her voice came out dangerously sweet, matching the precarious way her red lips pursed, "how's the situation going with the CJM student breakout? Any leads?"

"Ah, that, well—" He clicked his teeth, turning to face me. "Shouldn't we be more focused on these three, Your Loveliness? That godsforsaken dragon just killed hundreds of your illustrious students! And, they figured out the riddle by *cheating*, of all things!"

"Did they now?" the Enchantress questioned, grabbing her staff and toying with it in her hands as she stared at the sweating bubble man.

This is getting good, Benny whispered, *is there any more butter? Nothing better than free entertainment and butter.*

Benny, shut it.

"Enchantress, I don't know what these *imbeciles* have told you, but they're all lies. No students have been causing issues and this girl is most certainly just overexaggerating her circumstances so she can sully your perfect reputation."

"My perfect reputation? Oh, Nathaniel, you know as well as I that was ruined when the two-hundred-year-olds left three weeks ago," she retorted.

The two-hundred-year-olds? Benny questioned.

"Yes, Mistress, and we're doing our best to find them."

"Nathaniel," she stated, her voice going cold, a gust of wind ripping through the air, "this doesn't have to do with what happened between us all those centuries ago, does it?"

Nathaniel sputtered. "Mistress, that's just preposterous. I harbor no ill will towards you. Not then, not now, not ever!"

She shook her head, the cold wind accompanied by storm clouds forming above.

"Then you won't mind me doing *this.*"

Sticking her staff into Nathaniel—or was it Nathaniel's bubble? Magic made no godsdamn sense in this place—a spark of nebulous magic burst into the air, swirling around and around until it formed a glittering circle that looked like a mirror.

In the glittering mirror, an image of the Enchantress and Nathaniel popped up. They were in a sparkling meadow, his smile wide in his floating bubble. A large diamond ring sat in the Enchantress' hand. But when the image moved, the Enchantress was shaking her head, leaving the ring and Nathaniel in the meadow alone.

Rejected, Benny chuckled.

"Shh, I'm trying to watch," Gwenyth whispered.

Another image replaced the meadow, but it came and went as fast as a blur. And then another image, this one of Nathaniel selling lube to a group of sorceresses who laughed at him, Nathaniel's face growing red with anger. The Enchantress cursed under her breath, twisting her staff back and forth. With each twist, the images shifted rapidly, more and more of them flying through the magical mirror.

"This looks important," the Enchantress growled, locking her staff in place.

An image glittered into focus. It was Nathaniel in a luxuriously-decorated room with a horde of students. He was shouting at them, foam forming on his mouth and dribbling into his bubble.

"You all stay here under the iron fist of our idiotic Enchantress, learning the craft of how to make your so-called 'one true love' swoon," Nathaniel yelled at the CJM, "but I tell you this—those women do not deserve such effort from you. So, I offer you this instead: a chance to leave this ridiculous place. I've finally found a way to cause a break in the barrier without her permission, and I am using this knowledge for all your benefit. Take this opportunity and forge your own path! Don't be shackled by this academy for another day. Be with the women you desire and don't accept their rejection of you. Forge contracts and strike bargains to entrap them in your love! *Who's with me?*"

All the fae men erupted in shouts and cheers.

The Enchantress twisted her staff again.

Following the previous image, a new one appeared: the barrier opening, hundreds of fae men running into the forest, and Nathaniel cackling into the cold night air. The Enchantress didn't say a word as she removed her staff from Nathaniel's bubble. Magic collapsed and funneled back into him with a great whoosh.

Oh, I get it, Benny said, *Nathaniel's an incel!*

Breathing heavily, the Enchantress stood over Nathaniel's pathetic bubble.

"You disgust me," she seethed.

But Nathaniel floated up, looking down on her instead. "Those two-hundred-year-olds will ruin you and your precious academic reputation. A shame the fae prince was killed by the bounty hunter instead of successfully capturing this little princess here when he had the chance, but it's no matter. There's plenty of other CJM to do the work, and when they do, you'll no longer be able to manipulate men into spineless, doting failures. Because, while you promise true love, you yourself have never given it to those that deserve it!"

The Enchantress laughed. "To those who deserve it? Like you, Nathaniel? You're a godsdamn head in a floating bubble!"

"And if you had let me be yours, I could've been so much more," he sneered.

Angling her staff at him, she yelled an incantation. A burst of yellow light speared into him...

...but Nathaniel remained.

"Your magic can only touch me, not destroy me," he laughed, "so I'll get to watch as your students make heroes of themselves: abducting women, assaulting them, taking them as their own as they rightfully should. They owe them nothing! I owe you nothing!"

Hey Benny? I questioned. *Did you need another snack?*

A roar of glee resounded through our mental bridge as Benny opened his jaws nice and wide.

"This is what you get for denying my pursuits for your hand!" Nathaniel screamed, far too focused on his weird little revenge monologue to notice a huge ass dragon towering behind him. "You will know what it's like to be despised by all. You will finally feel the inferiority I've felt my whole life while being by your si—!"

Chomp.

And Nathaniel, the creepy incel bubble man, was no more.

9

ANYONE WANT SOME BAR-B-QUED WINGED MEN FOR DINNER?

I BIT into a jam-filled cookie while Gwenyth, Benny, and I followed the Enchantress through her grand castle. With her warden-turned-incel, Nathaniel, being eaten by Benny, she'd invited us for tea in her palace to further discuss the Chiseled-Jawed Men problem.

We still needed a plan to stop them from abducting Gwenyth. Then, we'd be able to return her home, and finally —*hopefully*—make it to the Butter and Barmaids Festival before it ended.

The thought of saying goodbye to Gwenyth caused me to pause, but I didn't let it sit.

The castle was huge, so huge that Benny was able to join us —so long as he kept his tail from swaying too much. Sapphires and rubies sat in silver encasings all over the walls, ceilings, and tiles, causing the space to feel like a fragile ornament.

But the decor was the least interesting part of the entire place.

I was most focused on the vast amount of fae men strolling in the hallway or behind closed doors performing tasks such as cooking and cleaning, or receiving what looked to be school lessons. Every single fae we passed couldn't keep their eyes off Gwenyth.

A part of me wanted to skewer every last one of them, but Gwenyth seemed to enjoy the attention, her cheeks turning pink while she occupied herself with curling a single finger in her hair.

Feeling jealous, Rhemy dearest? Benny asked into my mental bridge.

Gwenyth can do whatever she wants. It's not as if these guys have tried abducting her over the last week or anything.

Ok, I'm not trying to play love match here, but if you like her, maybe you should tell—

No.

Rhemy.

I sighed. *She's a princess, Benny. She's already arranged to marry someone when we return her. Whatever happened between us at the inn last night was just fun and games. Nothing more.*

Gwenyth turned to me, a gentle sparkle in her eye. I hated the way my cheeks flushed. And I especially hated the way her elbow brushed against mine and caused my arms to pimple.

Are you sure? Benny asked tentatively.

I—

"As a thank you for killing Nathaniel, I'd like to welcome you all to my grand castle," the Enchantress announced as she spread her arms wide. "This is where I teach fae men how to find their one true love! You've noticed by now they learn things such as simple house tasks, handiwork, and the like. Oh, and we can't forget that when they reach four hundred years old, they get to take the coveted anatomy and lust class."

A bit of cookie fell out of my mouth. "I'm sorry, did you say when they reach four hundred years old?"

I'm more stuck on the anatomy-and-lust-class part, Benny chimed in.

"Yes! Trust me, anytime before four hundred years and it's

too soon for them to take it seriously. They'll either forget all the knowledge of how to stimulate the clit or they'll just laugh at the fact anyone said the word 'clit'. It's very distracting and they're far less likely to win over their one true love without such knowledge."

Oh my gods.

"So let me get this straight: Nathaniel let out the two-hundred-year-olds, right?"

"Right," she agreed.

"And they're...?"

"Uncultured, bigoted, and enjoy junk food far more than wine tasting. Arguably the most difficult time for fae men in their maturing process. 'Terrible two-hundreds,' I like to call them."

I laughed so hard my stomach hurt. Benny joined me, his roar shaking the precariously hung chandeliers above us.

"You—" I paused, catching my breath, "you're telling us the reason these immortal men are always so damn old is because they aren't at their peak as a man? That they have to learn all this shit and it takes *hundreds* of years to do it?"

The Enchantress waved her staff. "This is a fact of nature. Fae men mature significantly slower than women, and they need exponential help until they can function as a partner instead of just as a child. My aim is to make sure women, like Gwenyth, can have partners who can satisfy their every need: physical, emotional, and even spiritual. This academy offers the perfect education to help these men and find and cherish their one true love."

And when are they ripe for the picking? Benny jested.

"Five hundred years old. On the day. I couldn't tell you why that is, but that's always when they're able to pass their final exams with flying colors. A day prior and they always fail."

Five hundred years? That's older than me!

I shook my head and finished my cookie. "Yet another reason why I love women."

Benny whipped his tail at me. I took it in the shoulder and playfully pushed him away.

The Enchantress raised her staff at Benny who quickly placed his tail between his legs.

Like everything else, the castle's south wing was beautiful. An array of green-and-gold velvet sofas were spread throughout the room, billiard tables and chess games peppered in the corners. Upstairs, there were so many doors I didn't even try to count them.

"This is only one out of ten common rooms for the terrible two hundreds. It comes complete with a wing specifically dedicated to the newest bardic releases where they can sing and dance while puking up their guts with hideous amount of tequila. I've learned there's no avoiding that stage, so it's best to let them get it out of their system and hopefully survive the alcohol poisoning."

"It really is like an academy," Gwenyth said, "but they're just learning to be... decent people?"

She nodded, running a hand along her wood staff. "Quite right. It's rigorous work, but I must say, the end results are truly magical. In fact, you've probably heard of our most popular chiseled-jawed man. His name is Rhy—"

Oh! What's this? Benny shouted into all our mental bridges.

In between his square-cut talons, Benny held one of the weirdest looking dildos I'd ever seen in my life. Three dicks, two spikes on the other end, and—gods—a tentacle coming out of its side.

"The Incinerator 4000!" Gwenyth exclaimed, rushing forward and looking at it with Benny. "I didn't know it'd released yet!"

"I get special accommodations to the newest gadgetry," the Enchantress smiled.

I thought you said anatomy and lust class wasn't until four hundred years, though? Benny said.

The magical woman shrugged. "Experimentation is also a poignant part of the process for the terrible two hundreds. And experiment they do, which is why I usually don't step within twenty feet of this wing. I'd be careful; their hygiene is still very questionable at this stage."

Benny dropped the dildo. Gwenyth jumped away.

Disgusting.

The Enchantress tapped her staff, "Anyways, back to business. I'm sorry for the problems they've been causing you all, especially you, Gwenyth." She paused, a small smile forming on her mouth. "You haven't found your fated mate, correct?"

Gwenyth's eyes widened. "Not that I know of."

"You would know if you did. Fae men are keenly attracted to young women in search of true love, especially when they're unmated." She tapped her staff again. "I have a plan that should get those two-hundred-year-olds back before sundown. But, your services will be required, Bounty Hunter."

Leaning an arm on Benny, I unsheathed my axe. "Now you're talking our language."

THE ENCHANTRESS WAS DECIDEDLY *NOT* TALKING our language.

What I'd assumed would be some epic, climatic battle against these dumb two-hundred-year-old fae men was actually just some trap that required Benny and me to make utter fools of ourselves.

Gwenyth was escorted to a room located at the highest point in the tallest part of the castle while Benny and I "guarded" it. Furrowing my brow, I read over the lines the Enchantress instructed me to yell:

> *This princess will die by my dragon's fire.*
> *She'll never be freed from this castle.*
> *The princess will be trapped within it's walls forever.*
> *My diabolical plan has finally worked and there's no escape.*
> *Reminder: buy more dildos for safe sex practice class. **AND DON'T*
> *FORGET THE ENCHANTED LUBE THIS TIME!*

"What in the literal *fuck*," I whispered, crumpling the piece of parchment in my fist. "This place can't be real."

Oh come on Rhema, it's kind of a fun idea, Benny replied, *and besides, all the CJM look so adorable in their little aprons.*

"I think I'm going to be sick."

If these were all women, you'd be having the best day of your life.

"And do you know why these aren't women? Because we don't need this kind of absurdness to function like a fully-formed human."

Mhmm, remind me again why you feel so betrayed by Rosanna taking the monster bounties?

I crumpled the paper harder.

And what about the way you stare at Gwenyth?

"Aren't you supposed to be roaring and breathing fire or something?"

Sounds like somebody needs a song.

A small smile tugged at my mouth as Benny's red eyes shimmered.

"Benny," I sighed, patting his scales, "please, do *not* sing—"

> *The steamy scent of cake baking in heat*
> *Yet ne'er so hot as what's underneath*
> *The aproned snake of a caked-up fae baker*
> *Baking a cake for his laid lady's favor*
> *Post-coidal fae baker baked layered cake*
> *For to gently awake for the laid lady's sake—*

Gwenyth's scream interrupted Benny's song. I wasn't sure if I could breathe when I caught sight of her, clad in a lavender-colored sheer dress. She leaned out the tower's window, pointing at me, and I realized she was cueing us. Since she did her job—screaming in terror—it was my turn to announce my diabolical plans for her.

According to the Enchantress, there was nothing more tantalizing to fae men than an unmated damsel in distress.

I wish I'd been burned to a crisp by Benny's fire instead.

"She'll never be freed from my clutches," I drawled, "the princess will die by my dragon's fire."

Benny and I soared into the sky and he let out a powerful roar, his flames spewing into the clouds.

This isn't going to work, I mumbled to him, *the Enchantress said there were hundreds of these guys. How in the hell are all of them going to just show up?*

"Gwenyth!" a deep male voice shouted from beyond the castle, "We're here to save you!"

Low and behold, an army of rippling-muscled fae men were storming the castle, the wizards and sorceresses screaming as they ran away from the barrier they'd been waiting and hoping to cross for who knows how long.

Pity.

But the fae men weren't filing into the correct wing like the Enchantress had hoped; instead, they were pillaging the place, and fighting and murdering the younger and older fae men wearing the cute aprons.

"Rhema! Benny!" the Enchantress shouted from below, her staff lit up and keeping back a group of CJM trying to grab her. "You've put on too convincing of a show! We're not going to survive this!"

"Who knew we'd be such a class act," I muttered. "Benny, ready for phase two?"

Always ready for phase two.

I smiled. *Then let's get to it.*

Ass up. Face down. Can't lose!

Turned out my wish to have a big climatic battle came true after all.

Winged men took to the skies and soared towards us, teeth bared and skin shining with sweat.

Anyone want some bar-b-qued winged men for dinner? Benny asked.

I'll take one. Not too overdone though.

Medium?

I prefer medium rare.

Excellent choice.

Fire erupted from his jaws, the heat searing my arms as the men shrieked and turned into ash. But a handful of them soared upwards, dodging the flames, piercing through the air and flanking us instead.

See you on the other side, I yelled into Benny's mind.

And then, I jumped onto one of the winged men.

He yelled, but my chokehold had him gagging on his spit. Stomach plummeting with our rapid descent, I unsheathed my axe and sliced into another man who was about to pierce me with his sword.

"Let Gwenyth go, you evil wretch!" the man I was choking yelled.

"To you? In your dreams."

His yell rumbled against my chest, and I laughed triumphantly as he flew us straight to Gwenyth's tower.

Perfect.

But my laughter was cut short when he rammed me into the castle wall. A deep groan shot out of me, all the air in my lungs gone. I kept my hold tight despite it, accompanying him on his wobbly flight path to Gwenyth's chamber. We made it to her window and I released my hold, pushing off him as I landed in her room.

"Gwenyth," the man shouted, "I'm here to mate with you."

I swung my axe as the fae flew in, slicing clean through his neck. His head rolled to the ground and his body thudded on the floor.

Gwenyth's puke landed on his eyes.

"Now *that's* disgusting," I cringed.

"I hate you so much."

"You weren't saying that last night."

Her face burned bright red, but before she could berate me, fae men with blond hair and green eyes rushed into the room.

"Gwenyth, we're here to—"

"Yeah, yeah, we know already."

Their screams died at the sharp edge of my axe-head. Blood splattered on my face, the beat of my heart thrumming hard and fast in my chest. Memories of war and corpses flooded my mind; I kept slicing and cutting and slicing and cutting.

Rhema, it's over! Benny yelled.

I stopped. More fae men were corralled at the door, but there was a deep fear in their eyes. They backed away until they disappeared down the stairs.

We did it, Benny continued, *the men who haven't been killed are headed back to their castle wing. The Enchantress says they're cooperating again and Gwenyth will be safe now.*

Taking a few long breaths, I gathered myself, sheathing my axe with a sharp clank.

Great, I replied. *Good work.*

I turned around. Gwenyth's eyes were wide, her skin a ghostly pale.

Opening my mouth to say something, I realized I didn't have any words. Dead bodies decorated my feet and blood dripped from my hands. I could see it in Gwenyth's gray eyes. I wasn't buying her a frilly coffee on a warm spring day or bantering with Benny about how he needed to wait patiently for his butter balls. I wasn't pretending to be tough until letting myself fall apart in her soft arms. Instead, I was a warrior fueled by years of relentless training, bloodied battles, and vengeance that had sunk its teeth into my heart.

Despite my late wife's similar gentle nature, she'd never looked at me the way Gwenyth did.

Like I was a monster.

"I just," Gwenyth paused, gulping, "I guess I forgot what you were capable of."

I rubbed the back of my neck. "I don't call myself a bounty hunter just for fun, Princess."

Silence stretched between us—heavy, solid—a type of finality snapping into it. Gwenyth darted her gaze to her feet, her shoulders sagging away from her ears.

"I want to go home," she whispered.

The tiniest piece of something in my chest cracked—but it didn't break.

"Then let's get you home, Gwenyth."

10

RIPE FOR THE PICKING

IT TOOK two days to fly back to the human realm. The saccharine sweet scent of the fae realm finally burned off with the brine of the sea. Gwenyth's kingdom sat perched on a cliffside next to the southern ocean.

This bounty job was finally over.

We could finally make it to the Butter and Barmaids Festival.

Thank gods.

"Benny, there's a clearing on the other side of the castle," Gwenyth pointed towards the sea, "we'll land there."

Alright, hold on tight, Benny warned.

We dipped through a cloud of mist, the seagulls squawking in the sky. Benny landed on the dry patch of dirt, the ground shaking beneath us. Sliding off Benny's back, I went to steady Gwenyth by her waist, but her knees didn't buckle this time.

Gwenyth smiled, placing her hands on mine. "Thank you, Rhema, for everything. I would've been a fae prince's locked up housewife for my entire life, if it hadn't been for you."

I couldn't help the small rush of heat in my face, my hands

still holding on to her waist. "Just don't go running off with any strange fae men again, alright?"

She scoffed. "You're insufferable."

"I try," I grinned, taking a deep breath and letting her familiar peony scent wash through me one last time.

We stood there for another moment, my hands on her hips and her hands on mine. Gwenyth's brows were drawn together, and her gray eyes didn't shimmer like they had over the past few days. A cold ache gripped my chest, like I was losing Emmaline all over again.

Then a warm memory fluttered through my eyes: Rosanna's touch. Her charming smile. Putting on our fighting leathers during the annual guild gatherings. How she talked about my bounty hunting like I inspired her despite how gloriously she could kill monsters without hesitation.

Rosanna.

She understood me in a way I hadn't realized.

Maybe this wasn't like losing Emmaline. Maybe I was getting something I wish I'd had all those years ago: a chance to say goodbye. A chance to start moving on.

Gwenyth seemed to notice my mind had gone somewhere else as she gently pressed a kiss on my cheek.

"You deserve a happily ever after too, you know?" she whispered.

I smirked. "I'll keep that in mind."

Letting go of each other, she turned to Benny.

"And Benny, I owe you at least a few pounds of butter before you leave."

Benny's eyes grew as wide as saucers. *Butter? Really? Oh boy, I would love that Gwenyth. Yes please, yes please, yes plea—*

A large gust of wind ripped through the air, the movement so harsh Gwenyth fell into my arms. We turned, confusion causing me to grab my axe. Dark mist swirled in a single spot on the dirt, a purple light emanating from its center.

"Get behind me," I instructed her.

A tall fae man stood before us, his black princely attire threaded with gold swirled patterns. He wore a smirk that made me want to smack it right off his chiseled face.

"I guess we missed one," I drawled, taking a step towards the chiseled-jawed man, "but don't worry, I'll end your life quickly."

The fae man laughed, his voice deep and rich. "You must be the bounty hunter, Rhema. The Enchantress told me much about you, mostly that I better behave accordingly or my head would be on the floor before I could get a chance to introduce myself."

I raised a brow. "The Enchantress? She sent you to meet me?"

"Well, I'm actually here for someone else."

His eyes glinted as his attention turned on Gwenyth.

"Oh no," the princess stepped back, "I'm not falling for this again."

The fae male bowed. "I understand others of my kind have treated you as if you were nothing more than an object. A disgusting, horrifying act. I'm sorry for what has happened to you because of their selfishness. But if you'd be so kind, I've been sent here by the Enchantress for my final exam."

"How so?" Gwenyth asked.

He stared deeply into her eyes. "To see if we're fated mates."

I groaned. "Are you fucking kidd—"

Rhema, hush.

Seriously? We just spent an entire week fighting these guys off of her, and now you're going to just let them have her anyways?

Benny's high-pitched whine pierced all our ears as he entered our mental bridges.

How old are you? Benny asked the fae.

Five hundred years old, he replied, *and a few days.*

Benny hummed. ***Ripe for the picking.***

Gwenyth gasped, taking a step towards him. As much as I wanted to stop her, I knew Benny's senses were keen about these things, and if this guy was actually the fully-matured version of a fae man...

Who was I to stop Gwenyth from taking back some control of her life?

"How would I know if we're fated mates?" she asked, taking another step towards him.

Eyes softening, the fae showed his palm. "If we touch hands, we'll know, for that which seeks its equal will find it."

Are my ears bleeding yet? I asked Benny.

Rhema, I'm trying to listen.

Gods, not you too.

Shhhhh.

Crossing my arms, I took a deep breath as Gwenyth tentatively approached the fae. He was handsome, that was for sure, but he stood different than the ones who'd been tracking her. There was a gentleness to him, a kind of serenity and depth as he held her gaze without flinching away.

If I didn't know better, I'd say he was in love.

We all held our breath as Gwenyth placed her palm on his.

Silence brushed by us with a light breeze. A seagull squawked in the distance. The fae's soft eyes started to burn with sadness, the emptiness in their touch seeming to cause him a kind of agony. I was surprised at how my chest ached watching them wait for something that wasn't there.

Like finding a letter after returning from a war, and learning your entire world had disappeared without so much as a whisper.

But then a purple light erupted from their hands.

Eyes wide and mouths gaping, Gwenyth and the fae man interlaced their fingers together, tears streaming down their faces as the light wisped around them, pulling them together and marking their hands with a swirled pattern that matched his attire. It felt like all the air had been taken out of existence and belonged only to them.

Then the light vanished.

Their markings remained.

Gwenyth smiled through her tears. "I feel like I've known you my whole life, and yet I don't even know your name."

The fae cupped her jaw, drawing her in close. "My name's Owain."

"Owain," she whispered back.

"I know this is all very sudden, so though everything inside of me is begging me to take you away and make sure nothing ever tears us apart, I need you to know that just because we're fated mates doesn't mean you need to choose this." He brushed his thumb along her hand. "To choose me."

I've got to hand it to him, even I'm melting a little bit.

I huffed a laugh, my vision blurring. *I guess those five hundred years really are the sweet spot.*

Gwenyth gripped the collar of his tunic. "Do you know how to eat a woman out? Or how to use the Incinerator 4000?"

I didn't mean for spit to fly out of my mouth, but it definitely did. And I definitely couldn't recover from it as Benny hit me in the back with his tail, attempting to stop my incessant choking.

Owain's grin turned feral. "I'd rather show than tell."

WEDDING BELLS ECHOED throughout the castle as Benny and I situated ourselves in the back of the church. The building was huge, the perfect height to accommodate Benny who was humming with the organs and chatting into my mind about how much he *loved* weddings.

Do dragons ever get married? I asked him.

Your human marriages are so informal and private, he replied, **we prefer to make our commitment to love as public as possible. Everyone's invited, not just friends and family, and as we mate on a freshly-laid bed of roses, everyone cheers us on—**

You know what? Forget I asked.

For someone who loves pleasuring yourself and others, I'm surprised how embarrassed you get by these things.

Benny, we're not having this conversation.

Thankfully I didn't have to hear his reply because the large doors opened and Gwenyth walked through with her father and mother. Apparently the King and Queen were so grateful to have Gwenyth back they quickly dismissed the pre-arranged marriage and allowed her to be with her fated mate instead.

That and his ability to create and maintain an impenetrable magic barrier around the kingdom certainly tipped the scales in his favor.

Gwenyth's wedding dress actually fit her this time around, no huge amounts of lace or ruffles threatening to eat her whole. Instead, she wore an intricate lace gown that hugged her small form. It was perfect.

Her five-hundred-year-old fae man, Owain, waited for her at the altar in his black attire with gold stitching.

Normally, I'd say meeting someone and getting married to them on the same day is only for insane people. But, even I couldn't deny the other-worldly connection these two experienced; and who was to say whether the magic made their love fake or real?

They said they cared for one other, and honestly, I believed them.

Half way through the ceremony, the officiant addressed the crowd:

"Are there any objections to this matrimony?"

Gwenyth shot me a mocking glare. I raised my hands in surrender—no more interrupting her wedding day. Laughing, she turned back to Owain, and the officiant pronounced them husband and wife.

11

BUTTER & BARMAIDS FESTIVAL

GOLD COIN WEIGHED heavy in my pocket as Benny and I entered the Butter and Barmaids Festival villa. Pink, green, and purple flags waved in the air, loose confetti sprinkling the gravel on which the hustle and bustle of all types of folks drank, sang, and laughed with one another.

Perfect.

There were still three whole days left of the Festival, which meant I could drink ale, buy more butter balls for Benny, and have some much-needed salacious fun.

But, to be honest, I wasn't all that horny anymore. The past week with Gwenyth and Rosanna had left me thinking more and more about my life before bounty hunting. And the more I thought about it—about my late wife who, even after all this time, I still missed like fucking crazy—the less inclined I felt to lose myself in a random woman I'd just met.

Maybe I'd just stick to drinking this time around.

Oh dear, would you look at the time, Benny exclaimed, *I need to go see about overhauling an amphitheater to make sure I can sing my new set of songs!*

Hold on, I grabbed his reins, *I thought you wanted butter balls the minute we got here?*

What makes you say that?

Because you couldn't shut up about it until five minutes ago.

Uh, right, we can do it later? I really need to go!

Benny, I warned, *what did you do?*

Me? Nothing! I did nothi—

"Rhem!" a familiar, feminine voice called.

I turned around. Rosanna's long, braided hair swayed in the breeze, her thigh-high boots and exposed midriff covered in blood. She carried three pints of ale between her hands. Her bright smile gleamed against the sun, her familiar dark-brown skin a sight for sore eyes.

All the anger I had been harboring from the monster bounty fiasco flew somewhere outside the Butter and Barmaids Festival walls. Benny had been right—maybe if I told her how I felt, that I was hurt because I'd grown to care about her, then we could put it behind us.

Oh, would you look at that, Rosanna's here! What a coincidence.

Benny, go sing your songs before I murder you.

He dashed away, but before the mental link was severed, I tapped on it.

Thanks, bud.

Love you too, Rhemy, he replied.

I smiled, greeting Rosanna with a snarky comment and immediately falling into a bet with her and some friends she'd made about who could finish their pint of ale fastest. She poked at me during the whole thing, jeering about how she was a better fighter than me while I argued I was a better riddlemaster than her.

"Rosanna," I said after a giant gulp of ale, leaning so close I could smell her cardamom-and-leather scent and the beer on her lips, "I'm sorry."

"Sorry?" Rosanna laughed, clinking her glass with mine and eyeing my fingers. "What in the hells are you talking about?"

"The monster bounty spot," I replied. "I was jealous. I wanted those bounties but you got them instead."

"Oh, that," Rosanna paused. "Look, Rhem, you don't need to apologize. It's just that I couldn't stay in the human quadrant anymore. You've got a gift I can't quite seem to find."

"What's that?"

She shook her head. "It's embarrassing."

I hit her shoulder. "I can't be honest with you and then you give me nothing back. It's not how this whole... communication business works."

"Communication business?" She laughed, taking a long drink. "Alright then: but you have to promise you won't tell anyone in the guild."

I crossed my heart with my hand.

"I can't kill people," she said.

My smile vanished.

"Or, at least, I can't stomach it, whether they're human, fae, you name it," she continued, "But I didn't want to leave the guild, so I needed to be in a monster quadrant. I guess I just never quite knew how to say it. "

Turning to me, her brown eyes glimmered.

Dammit all. This whole time I'd been so upset about not getting what I'd wanted that I hadn't considered her life outside of fucking around with my emotions. Maybe I should've taken a course at that Enchantress' weird-ass academy. Did they have a "how to not be an asshole" basic training?

"I wouldn't call the ability to kill people a gift," I muttered.

"It is when they're bent on using their power to hurt others. You kill, Rhem, but you save, too. It's what I admire about you." She brushed her arm against mine.

Face heating and drink rushing to my head, I laughed. All I

wanted was to offer an apology but instead I was imagining her lips on mine, her hips grinding against my body–

"Hope that was honest enough for you," Rosanna said, leaving my skin cold and taking a deep drink, the glimmer in her eyes gone.

She's not interested.

Gods, how many times did I misread our interactions this past year? Clearly too many to count.

"Right, yeah, of course," I replied with a hiccup. "Just as long as you don't beat me in the guild's annual kill count, then I'm fine staying in the immortal quadrant."

Rosanna's smile turned devilish. "Oh, but I'm already thirteen bodies ahead of you."

I dropped my pint on the table with a loud thud and pushed away from her. "That's impossible. Benny and I just killed hundreds fae men!"

"Ah yes, that's an impressive count, but I'm thirteen ahead of you thanks to a species of monstrous crabs that were able to multiply whenever their shell came in contact with water; I'm winning that trophy this year." She poked my nose with her finger. "And you won't be able to stop me."

"In your *dreams*," I growled, shoving her hand away.

Her smile and laughter filled the festival tent, Benny's voice accompanying hers as he sang one of his new songs.

We continued to argue about who was going to win the kill count award. Even more so, we argued about who had the best bounty hunter story from the past year.

Obviously, it was the one where Benny and I saved a princess from a fae prince.

The En—

*R*HEMA, *I want to say goodbye to them.*

Goodbye to who, Benny?

That person! The one who's looking at our thoughts on this page.

How in the hells can you see them?

Please, Rhema, can I say goodbye?

Oh my gods, fine, just make it quick.

You there, reading this page—yes, you! Thank you for reading our story about this... well, this very odd adventure in the fae realm. We've documented many, many other adventures in the different realms where we save women from immortals, and I can't wait for you to read those ones too! Oh, and if you know anyone who's looking to produce songs, it would mean a lot if you put in a good word for me—

That's it, you're done.

Wait, Rhema!

Goodbye and have a good night. We'll see you all on our next adventure.

ACKNOWLEDGMENTS

This story was an absolute fever dream that came to me when I was sitting in the bathtub on a random Tuesday night in March. I'd been agonizing over the concept of a buddy/cop duo since August 2025 and just couldn't pinpoint where Rhema & Benny could fit in a romantasy story plotline. And then BING. Bathtub inspo. I immediately texted my spouse my idea and his response was: PERFECTION.

Paul, thank you for being the funniest person I swear I've ever met. You're crazy-ass ideas were not trashed this time around because this was an unserious story (unlike my debut). We had some really fun, silly conversations about this piece that I'm going to cherish forever. Thanks for being my person.

Forever grateful for my writing group at Bardsy. Adam Simon—thank you for (not so gently) spurring me on to stick to what I'd originally intended this story to be: a comedy. It was hard some days to find the ability to laugh, but this story pushed me in surprising ways. Thank you to Allie Oleander, Samantha Traina, Joey Coleman, Lynda Melbane White, Kimberly Straub, C.C. Tyler, & Justin Chesney. You all showered Benny with so much love and helped me figure out who the hell Rhema was meant to be.

And a big, big thank you to my beta readers: Sofi, Teah, Grace, and Katy. Your feedback comments had me howling into the night. It was a joy and an honor to get your feedback on this zany little story. To my incredible fantasy and romantasy critique partners: Alex Bree, K.C Woodruff, Tiffany O'Haro, Jaci

M. Lunera—thank you for catching some very major problems that could've resulted in me being arrested (ok, exaggeration, but still) as well as adding some prime time comedy elements that made this story even funnier.

And, of course, my partner-in-crime Jackie Snow—you were the second person I messaged about this crazy novella idea and you also knew this direction for the story *was it*. Being able to knock this story out during our birthday weekend together in a secluded cabin with our spouses waiting on us hand-and-foot was the epitome of "writer life". Let's do another writing retreat soon.

Of course, I'd be a fool to not give all the flowers my wonderful editor Ashley Postman-Keller (Aspen Editorial) deserves. Thank you, yet again, Ashley, for cleaning up my grammar messes and turning them into gold. I always know you'll be there to save the day from my ridiculous punctuation errors (Why Do I Capitalize Everything?) and sentence structure guffaws. Plus you make me feel like a million bucks with your praises. Grateful simply doesn't cover it.

Last but most certainly not least, thank you reader. This story was made for you, first and foremost, as a fun spoof on our dearest beloved romantasy genre. I hope you enjoyed it in all of its weird and wild takes on some of our favorite tropes. Benny and Rhema will return again soon!

ABOUT THE AUTHOR

With a master's degree in social work, A.J. Braun finds a deep fascination in how people make sense of their world, relationships, and themselves. This, in combination with their deep love for the fantasy and romance genres, inspired Braun to tell their own romantasy stories. When they're not pouring over their manuscripts, you can also find Braun hanging out with their spouse and friends, cuddling their two black cats, participating in local sport leagues, and playing D&D into the wee hours of the night.

9 798990 705449